Fierce Femmes *and* Notorious Liars

A DANGEROUS TRANS GIRL'S CONFABULOUS MEMOIR

Fierce Femmes and Notorious Liars

A DANGEROUS TRANS GIRL'S CONFABULOUS MEMOIR

— Kai Cheng Thom —

METONYMY PRESS

Montreal, QC

This is a work of fiction. Names, characters, events, and incidents are either the products of the author's imagination or used in a fictitious manner. Any resemblance to actual persons, living or dead, or actual events is purely coincidental.

First edition
Printed and bound in Canada by Imprimerie Gauvin
Cover design and artwork by Samantha Garritano
Proofreading by Jenn Harris / Lucid Pulp
Ninth printing - 2021

Published by Metonymy Press
PO Box 143 BP Saint-Dominique
Montreal, QC H2S 3K6
Canada
metonymypress.com

Library and Archives Canada Cataloguing in Publication

Thom, Kai Cheng, author
       Fierce femmes and notorious liars : a dangerous trans girl's confabulous memoir / Kai Cheng Thom.

ISBN 978-0-9940471-3-7 (paperback)

       I. Title.

PS8639.H559F54 2016   jC813'.6   C2016-906998-2

For my family, blood and chosen. And for fierce femmes,
fighters, haunted girls, and liars everywhere.

Dangerous stories

I don't believe in safe spaces. They don't exist. I do, however, believe in dangerous stories: The kind that swirl up from inside you when you least expect it, like the voice of a mad angel whispering of the revolution you are about to unleash. Stories that bend and twist the air as they crackle off your tongue, making you shimmer with glamour, so that everyone around you hangs on to your every intoxicating word. The kind of stories that quiet mad girls dream of to bring themselves comfort after crying themselves to sleep at night, that made your poor starving grandfather cross an entire ocean in search of the unbelievable riches someone once told him were waiting on the other side.

The kind of story that doesn't wait for you to invite it to enter, but bursts through the doors of your rat-infested house like a glittering wind, hungry, hungry, to snatch up the carpet and scatter your papers and smash every single plate in the kitchen. That surges, howling, up the battered stairs to blast the stained sheets off your filthy bed and sweep your secrets out of the closet and send them shrieking outside, overjoyed to be finally set free.

Where are those kinds of stories about trans girls like you and me?

The other day I was watching some post-sex television when a beautiful white trans woman in a flowy white organza gown appeared on the screen. She was making a speech. Everything about her was very white, like she was about to be buried and crushed into a diamond. She was already a multi-millionaire celebrity from before she came out, and when she did everyone made a big deal about it. Then she got The Surgery, and now she's getting an Upstanding Good Samaritan Pillar of the Community Award for, like, being brave or whatever.

Which is actually pretty cool, I guess, because good for her, you know? Though I will admit to being just the teeniest bit jealous, because I have always wanted a flowy dress like that. But I'm not hating on her for being rich or famous or white or anything (not much, anyway).

No, what really works me up is the *way* that this whole story is being told: Everyone look at this poor little trans girl desperate for a ~~fairy godmother~~doctor to give her boobs and a vagina and a pretty face and wear nice dresses! Save the trans girls! Save the whales! Put them in a zoo!

It's actually a very old archetype that trans girl stories get put into: this sort of tragic, plucky-little-orphan character who is just supposed to suffer through everything and wait, and if you're good and brave and patient (and white and rich) enough, then you get the big reward ... which is that you get to be just like everybody else who is white and rich and boring. And then you marry the prince or the football player and live boringly ever after. We're like Cinderella, waiting to go to the ball. Like the Little Mermaid, getting her tail surgically altered and her voice removed, so that she can walk around on land. Those are the stories we get, these days.

Or, you know, ones where we're dead.

Where are all the stories about little swarthy-skinned robber trans girls waving tiny knives made of bone? About trans teenage witches with golden eyes who cut out their own hearts and lock them in boxes so that awful guys on the internet will never break them again? About trans girls who lost their father in the war and their mother to disease, and who go forth to find where Death lives and make him give them back?

Looking at the ivory face of the trans lady on the TV, I decided then and there that someone had to write us girls a dangerous story: a transgender memoir, but not like most of the 11,378 transgender memoirs out there, which are just regurgitations of the same old story that makes us boring and dead and *safe* to read about. I wanted something kick-ass and intense with hot sex and gang violence and maybe zombies and lots of magic.

Which is, you know, pretty much my life, right? So I thought I'd give writing a try.

The crowd gave a standing ovation as the millionaire trans lady on TV finished her speech about believing in yourself, and the 127 percent of transgender teenagers attempting suicide, and how we need to support them in their struggle to wait for things to Get Better. I felt this hot spiky anger, like I wanted to kick right through the television screen. Right through her stupid Botox pasty face. And I would have done it too. It was my boyfriend's television, and he's got a good job and everything, and I could have said my foot slipped.

But ultimately, I just couldn't. Because at the end of the day, she's still my sister, you know? And as much as I don't like her or am jealous or whatever, I still feel the need to keep the sister love flame burning inside my heart. I don't want to become one of those old bitter activist types who has to hate everything.

So instead of kicking, I blew a kiss at the TV. A spark jumped from my lips, skipped off my palm, and darted through the air to touch down gently on a close-up of her face. The screen exploded in a glorious symphony of electricity and shattering glass, and a thousand razor shards flew through the air and turned into crimson butterflies that danced through the room on their way out the window.

PART I: RUNAWAY

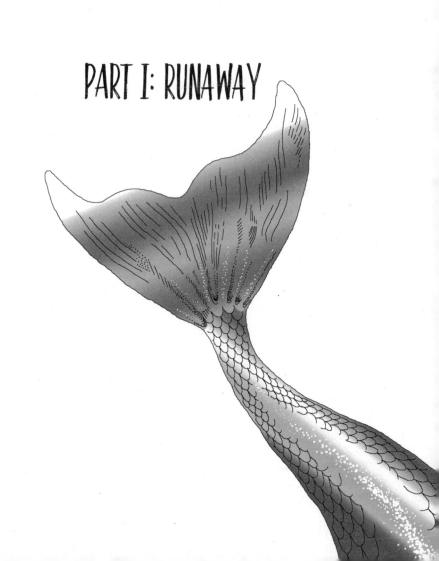

The crooked house in the heart of Gloom

This is the story of how I became a dangerous girl and the greatest escape artist in the world.

I grew up in a crooked house in a place called Gloom, where the sky is always grey and the rain is always falling. Gloom was built on the edge of the sea, on land that was once inhabited solely by several Indigenous nations to whose peoples the land and the water are sacred. For thousands of years they lived in this place without external invasion, until white people came from Europe with guns and diseases and their hearts full of conquest. These white people built a city of stone and glass as a monument to their victory, and because they had won it in so corrupt a fashion, the sky and the ocean have been sad ever since.

This is why the city is called Gloom.

I was born in the crooked house whose walls curved and bulged in the middle and narrowed at the top and the bottom, like a starving person with a swollen belly. My parents were both immigrants from China. My mother was a former pop music starlet in Hong Kong who dreamed of singing in America, and my father was a disciple in a Shaolin temple, which he left to follow her. It's a very romantic story, but unfortunately this is all I ever heard of it. By the time I was born, all they had in common were their broken dreams, an unpaid mortgage, and an ever-present feeling of hunger.

My parents had been hungry for so long that it filtered into all of their emotions and all of their dreams. They saw the world through hunger-tinted glasses, so that every plate looked a little less full of food than it really was and every paycheque (never large enough to begin with) seemed even smaller. When they looked at me and my sister, even their love was hungry.

Their greatest hopes rested on me, because I was a boy. They knew that here, as in China, a boy stood the best chance of getting a good job. They wanted this stability for me, which they had never had themselves. And perhaps a small part of them hoped that I would bring them prosperity as well.

It's not wrong to hope, my mother always said. It is never wrong to hope.

Hope made my parents fearful that I might get sick and die or be kidnapped at any moment. Hope made them wary of television or toys or friendship or anything else that might distract me from getting good grades and going to university. Hope kept me trapped in the belly of the crooked house, in a tiny bedroom, surrounded by books instead of people.

It wasn't so bad, really. Had I been more studious, or more filial, I might have been content with this life. Except for two things that threw a monkey wrench into my parents' carefully devised plans: I was always wild at heart, and I wanted to be a girl.

So I crept out of the house instead of poring over my books, and I failed spelling tests and math quizzes at school, and I put my mother's black stockings over my head and pretended they were a princess's long, long hair. The more I defied them, the harder my parents tried to hold on to me. They spanked me with a wooden spoon and shouted that I was bad and ungrateful, and they put locks on the doors and windows of the crooked house.

But, like I said, I was wild at heart. So I continued to refuse to study my books and instead spent the time learning to pick locks.

Picking locks is a glorious thing. To be able to open sealed doors is the greatest and most important kind of magic, because it allows you to interact with the world on your own terms. If I were Prime Minister (Prime Ministress?), I would have it taught in all elementary schools, with an option for advanced study at the upper levels of education.

At night, when my parents were asleep, dead tired from their dead-end factory jobs, I would pick the lock on my bedroom window and ease the panes open. I'd tie my bedsheets into a rope and rappel down the wall of the crooked house.

I'd slip away into the darkness and run off to the nearby playground, which the city had stopped caring for long ago. The whole structure was overrun with weeds, the wooden jungle gym rotted and collapsed. People often used this park to shoot up, and I had to be vigilant to avoid leftover needles. But there was a rusty metal swing set there, and I would jump up on a swing (standing, not sitting) and hurl my feet toward the heavens as if I knew I could fly.

On those nights, the stars were only pinpricks through the clouds. Bats would flutter overhead. The family of mangy three-legged coyotes that roamed our neighbourhood would yip and howl, and I would feel my whole body clenching up with hungry hope as I planned my Great Escape.

The day the mermaids died

I decided it was time to leave on the day the mermaids died. For as long as anyone could remember, a school of mermaids had made their home in the gulf off the coast upon which the city of Gloom stood. They often swam into the harbour, to sing their songs and trade flirtatious glances with sailors. On this particular day, however, the entire mer-clan surged up to the edge of the shore during high tide and heaved their bodies onto the sand, beaching themselves. All along the sand they lay, over sixty dying mermaids, even the smallest of them nearly as long as an oil tanker, gurgling out their funeral dirge.

To this day, not a single scientist has come up with an explanation for this—except, of course, that we had poisoned the seas with our oil and trash, and that it was the end of the world, which everyone knew already.

I decided to skip school that day—it was my senior year, so the teachers didn't care, being even more burned out than we were—and join the volunteer rescue crew that was desperately trying to save them. It was almost definitely hopeless, because mermaids cannot last more than a few hours out of water, but some people just can't stop themselves from trying to hold on to what's already been lost. Some people will cling on to anything that makes them feel even a little bit free.

When I was little, watching the mermaids, even just knowing that they were out there, made me feel like maybe anything was possible. I nabbed my little sister out of her sixth-grade class too, so that I could say goodbye. It was easy. I just said we had "urgent family business" and we walked out, totally unscathed.

My sister's name is Charity, which I think suits her perfectly. She's always been tiny for her age, and has waist-length hair and these enormous eyes that make her look like an anime character. She's the sweetest person I have ever known, but she was already starting to change on the cusp of teenhood. She was becoming hungrier, harder around the edges. No one could grow up in Gloom, with a family like ours, and remain completely innocent.

She was thrilled to get out of school and get on the bus with me. I took her out on these little field trips fairly regularly and we always had a great time. Her favourite was the Royal Taxidermy Museum downtown, and mine was the Aquarium, which tells you a lot about the two of us. I knew she was going to be sad when I told her I was going away.

When we got to the beach, there was already a group of thirty people there, running back and forth with buckets of sea water, trying to keep the mermaids wet until the tide came back. A few were attempting to haul a mermaid back into the ocean, but it wasn't going well. The average mermaid weighs seven tons and is nearly dead weight on the land. The sky was grey, like it always is in Gloom, and the air was filled with the stench of the sea and dying flesh and the farewell songs of the mermaids—a sonorous, wordless keening.

We chose the mermaid who looked the most lively, and started hustling with two buckets each. It didn't look good for her, to tell the truth. Already the turquoise scales of her tail were beginning to flake off and fall onto the sand. Her seaweed-coloured hair was a fading tangled mass, and she looked at us with huge golden eyes that never blinked. The gills at the sides of her head fluttered slowly, making a rattling, hissing noise that sounded like death itself. She didn't look scared.

"I'm going to leave town soon," I said to my sister, as we filled up our buckets with brine. Charity nodded, like *yeah, yeah.*

"I'm serious," I said. "I'm going away to become a woman. I've always felt uncomfortable as a boy, and you know Mom and Dad are never going to be into it. So I'm leaving tomorrow."

Charity didn't say anything, just picked up her buckets and started lugging them back to the mermaid. I could see she was trying to walk fast, put some distance between herself and me, but like I said, she's a tiny girl, so she wasn't really getting anywhere.

"I'm sorry to just spring it on you like this," I said. "I didn't want to freak you out."

"I'm not freaked out," she said. But her voice was a little trembly, so I didn't say anything for a while. We splashed the sea water over the mermaid, and then we went back and forth a few more times.

"I'll write you emails all the time," I said, trying to keep my own voice steady, but my throat was all knotted up. "And I'll send you postcards, and pretty rocks, and the wings of dead birds I find lying on the road for your collection."

"I don't want any of those things," my sister said. Her voice was all tremble now.

"Oh," I said. And then, "I'm sorry."

"You don't have to be sorry," she said. "I'm not sad because you didn't tell me, or because you're going away, or because you're becoming a girl. I'm sad because you're not taking me with you. Are you?"

And there it was: the real reason why I hadn't told her earlier that I was leaving. It wasn't because I was trying to spare her feelings. It was because I was selfish. Because I wanted to escape, really escape, and to do that I had to run away into a world where she could not follow.

"Where I'm going is too dangerous, Charity," I said. But it had the coppery taste of a half-truth, and we both knew it.

She nodded. "I know," she said, and I was crying now, on this stinking beach between the grey sky and the grey sea. I was thinking about the day she was born. My father had placed her in my arms, and suddenly I wasn't alone anymore in that crooked tiny house in the heart of Gloom.

"What'll I do?" she whispered, and then she was lunging at me and pounding me with her tiny fists. "What'll I do? What'll I do?"

I caught her hands in mine and pulled her close to me, wrapping my arms around her so that she could not strike, so that we could feel each other's heartbeat. When she was very small, she used to have tantrums where she would scream and pound the floor, and I would hold her just like this.

And right then, the mermaid, who had been completely still until this moment, lifted her enormous fleshy arm and, with vocal cords never meant for human speech, said, "Eeeeerrrrggghhhnuuuurrgghfff." Her voice sounded like crashing waves.

My sister and I both turned toward her, shocked. While mermaids often interacted with humans, they were never known to speak to us. No one was even really sure whether they understood our languages.

"Did she say ... *enough*?" Charity said.

"Eeerrrrrggghhhnuuuugghhff," said the mermaid again, and she was smiling a little now, looking right into our eyes with the golden gaze of a being so ancient and so forgiving that it made me want to disappear. "Thaaaaargghhhnnnnk yeeeuuuurrrrghhhh," she sighed.

And all over the beach, the rest of the mermaids were thanking the humans who were trying to save them, and telling them *enough*. There was nothing we could do now to fix the mistakes we had made.

And then the mermaid at our feet raised her voice in a great ululating cry that shook the air and vibrated in our bones, and one by one the rest of the mermaids took up the chorus. For a terrible minute it felt like the whole world was coming undone at the sound of their voices, and then the song finally faded, and the mermaids were all gone.

The lesson of the bees

There are some things that even the most dangerous girl in the world can't fight. It doesn't matter how strong or smart or well-prepared you are. Sometimes all you can do is stay perfectly still and surrender to something that is greater than you. I learned this from the bees.

It happened on a summer afternoon when the sky was blue, which is rare in the city of Gloom. I was six. I was supposed to be reading quietly in my room, like always, but I couldn't resist the urge to slip out the window, shimmy down the brick wall, and run off to play in our neighbour Old Man Tom's garden.

I don't even know what I was playing—one of those nonsensical imagination games that little kids like so much. Pretending I was a princess riding a unicorn into battle against the Shadow Army, maybe. Old Man Tom's garden was perfect for games like that, because it wasn't really a garden so much as a jungled snarl of vines and spiky shrubs and sticky orange flowers that dripped a sweet-smelling clear liquid.

I should have been tipped off by the noise. I should have known to stay away from that clump of vines. But I've always been reckless. Maybe I thought they would make a good hideout for my princess character. I pushed my way into the vines and fell into a world of bees.

The air erupted with buzzing. Fat golden honeybees swirled around me in a furious cloud, landing in my hair, on my skin. Jolts of terror shot through me wherever their tiny legs touched. My body reacted without conscious control, somehow knowing exactly what to do: nothing. I froze, barely breathed. I screwed my eyes shut and prayed, prayed to the roaring swarm, *forgive me.*

I don't know how long I kneeled there, immobile. Minutes or hours could have passed as the insects decided my fate. My muscles cramped and my back ached, but I did not move. Little by little, the bees and I made peace. When I finally uncoiled, one inch at a time, and walked into the sunlight, I had not been stung even once.

Wait. Sorry. That's not what happened. Here is what happened:

On a cold winter evening, my mother opened the door to the back porch of the crooked house so she could smoke a cigarette. A swarm of killer bees raced past her, and because it was night and she was exhausted from working in the candle factory, she did not notice them. Or maybe she just didn't care.

Into the house they swirled, a boiling cloud of rage and desire, searching for the sweetest, softest thing they could find. I lay, six years old, in my bed in my tiny room, and they flooded inside through the crack under the door.

They landed on me, covered me with their vibrating bodies, crawled inside my lips and up my nostrils, into every orifice, and they drank up all the nectar they could hold. I did not move, did not scream, because I knew that if I did, I would be stung into oblivion.

Instead I lay there, clutching the sheets in my fists, and waited for it to be over. I prayed to the ravenous swarm, *forgive me*. And at last, they were finished. They lifted themselves up on their wings and flew off into the night.

Except. Some of them stayed. Addicted to my sweet blood, they crawled up inside my body and built their nests there. They are still inside me. They will always be.

from my notebook —

song of the pocket knife, part 1

i have a small silver friend
that I keep with me always:
in the pocket of my jeans,
or the waistband of my skirt,
the lower left pocket
on the outside of my backpack.
my pocket knife
is a very good friend:
small, silver, reliable,
and unlike me,
it always tells the truth.
and sometimes,
when there are too many insects –
angry – alive – wriggling – under my skin,
i take my pocket knife and
open up mouths in my skin
to try
and let them
out.

City of Smoke and Lights

West of the ocean and east of the wind, there is a place they call the City of Smoke and Lights. The streets are crooked, and the light is heavy, and the air is stained ash grey from the glamorous cigarette lips of hungry ghosts swimming through the fog.

In the City of Smoke and Lights, they say, anything can happen if you dream it. As soon as a tall tale leaves your wicked mouth, it falls to the ground, moist and warm, wriggling with thick possibility. It sinks in deep, puts down roots. Splits the pavement as it rises, tall and spindly.

You can be anyone. They say. In the City of Smoke and Lights. The rent is cheap and the streets are lean and people are crazy as anything hell could spit out. You can be anything you want: baller, biker, bad girl, punk rocker, faerie queen, goth, artist, stoner, vampire, dominant, submissive, witch, man, woman, medusa, monster, mother, poet, demon, lost boi, foxfire phantom gleaming out of the night, superhero, goddess, strong, beautiful, powerful, untouchable, whole. In the City of Smoke and Lights.

You can be the mango sweet golden skin woman swinging her hips to the bass at three in the morning, or the androgynous skeleton running cold bone hands through the sweat of her hair.

You can be lizard slinker leather jacket man loping through a shard-strewn alleyway, or befeathered queen in sequined high heels waving from the open back door.

You can be a changeling child, skin blossoming hot then blowing cold to the rhythms of the drumbeat moon, refusing to decide who to fuck or when to become.

So I'm taking all the cash I've been able to save or steal and spending it on a one-way ticket on a rickety bus that looks like an oversized soft-drink can. Packing all my essentials into my raggedy backpack: a couple of outfits, lipstick, the pocket knife that I keep with me always, the notebooks in which I write down little bits of stories and wishes and interesting nightmares. I'm saying goodbye to everything else, to the school books in my room and the swing set in the park behind my parents' house. To coyote songs and the silver-grey sky of Gloom.

I get on the bus and find myself a seat, way in the back, that smells like old cigarettes and is slightly sticky. Slouch down so nobody will look at me. Sometimes, to become somebody else, you have to become nobody first.

You have to let go of your mother and father, the crooked starving house you grew up in that wanted to devour you and digest you whole. Forget, if you can, all the promises you've made and the lies that you've told.

Forget the scars you left one, two, three times on your left wrist. Forget flowers and killer bees and everyone you've ever known.

In the City of Smoke and Lights, they say, you can be everything you dreamed of. Especially if you are prone to nightmares, deep and wild. So I'm going to find the place where my shadow ends and my body begins. Close your eyes. I'll see you there.

Ghost Friend, or, The only person who can make me come

As the pop-can bus bounces and groans down the highway, I feel the faintest caress of ghostly fingers on my shoulder. A slight tingle, as though someone not quite there is breathing on my cheek.

I have this problem, which is sort of embarrassing. It's that there is only one person I've ever met who can make me orgasm, and that person is a ghost. No joke. Their name is Ghost Friend, or at least that's what I call them. I don't know what their real name is, or what gender they identify with, because they don't talk.

I met Ghost Friend one day when I was skipping school in the eleventh grade so that I could go have a picnic in the local cemetery. I realize how emo that sounds, but I swear it wasn't because of any sort of affinity for tombstones. It's because there was this really amazing fried chicken place across the street from the graveyard, and the Korean lady who ran it sometimes gave me leftovers from the lunch rush for free. She said I reminded her of her granddaughter, because of my long hair. How great is that? She was the only person in those days who recognized my womanhood.

And the cemetery was the only quiet and beautiful place in the middle of the city to sit and eat fried chicken.

So I was sitting on a memorial bench, contemplating the wings of a stone statue and enjoying my lunch, when I felt a hand on my shoulder. I whirled around, grabbing frantically for the pocket knife I always kept in my jeans, but of course I saw no one there. And then the hand touched my shoulder again.

This happened a few more times before I realized that I was being contacted by a ghost. At first, I trembled and grabbed my lunch to leave, but that gentle hand landed on my shoulder again and—well. You have to understand, there wasn't a whole lot of excitement in my life. Or companionship.

And Ghost Friend wasn't at all threatening. I could tell right away, even though they're invisible and mute. There was just something about the way they touched me—gentle, tentative, almost apologetic. Like a warm breeze, if breezes had fingers. And I realized that Ghost Friend was shy.

We developed a system of communication, unimaginative but effective nonetheless: I would ask Ghost Friend a question. They would tap my shoulder in response. One tap for yes. Two for no. And sometimes we would abandon this system altogether in favour of a more sensory, primal form of communication.

"Are you a ghost?"

One tap.

"Are you here to hurt me?"

Two taps.

"Are you haunting me?"

No response.

"Do you want to be my friend?"

One tap.

"So, what do you want to do?"

A gentle caress around the back of my neck and over my collarbone, sliding up my throat to cup my chin. Then the ghostly hand was gone, abruptly, as though frightened by its own boldness.

"You can do that again if you want."

The caress happened once more, but slower this time. Like silk dragging across velvet. Slow and warm and full of meaning.

"You can touch my hair."

"You can touch my shoulders."

"You can touch my chest."

"You can touch my thighs..."

Ghost Friend explored all of my tender parts, one by one. And I felt heat rising, quickening, and fizzing under my skin. I had tried sex before, with a few boys and one girl at school. It had always ended badly—with the sensation of dark black bees buzzing and wriggling inside me, wherever I was touched, reminding me of what had happened.

But Ghost Friend was so slow, so barely substantial, so responsive to my direction, that the bees and buzzing and wriggling did not come. And for the first time since that terrible night of the killer bees, I was able to feel the pleasant, slightly shameful feeling I had been longing for.

"You can reach under my shirt," I whispered. "You can touch inside my pants."

And anyone driving by the cemetery and looking in would have seen a crazy Asian boy muttering to himself and having a spontaneous orgasm while thrashing about on top of a memorial bench. But really, I was a girl being miraculously touched by a ghost.

Ghost Friend followed me home after that. On some nights when I am lonely, I feel them tap me on the shoulder. They never go further without my spoken permission, no matter how many times we've played this game. Sometimes I can feel them warning me, tugging me out of the path of danger, or sometimes they comfort me when I am sad. I love Ghost Friend, or at least as much as you can love someone who has no body and no voice.

I was worried that I might leave Ghost Friend behind, along with the phantom orgasms they give me, when I made my escape from Gloom. But now that I'm on a bus a thousand miles from home, I feel those ghostly fingers again, brushing against my shoulders like flower petals. I guess my Ghost Friend is still here, haunting me. Giving me orgasms that no one else can. This makes me happy, but in a sad kind of way, because I know that a part of me will always want for something more.

How to kill a man with your bare hands

There's a man on this bus who keeps looking at me like I'm a piece of meat. He's got a shaved head and a bunch of bicep tattoos, and I can tell he thinks he's hot stuff. He won't stop turning around to stare at me with this vaguely menacing look, like he's considering eating me. I'm wearing my black boots, a black miniskirt, and a lacy black top. Most of the ten or so other passengers haven't even given me a second glance, but I know this guy can tell I'm trans. Trans and travelling alone on a bus in the middle of Nowhere at 3 a.m.

When the bus pulls over for a two-hour break, I get out to stretch my legs. The stop is basically a gigantic twenty-four-hour gas station on the side of the highway with a couple sad-looking fast-food stands and tables attached. I buy a pack of cigarettes, then walk around the perimeter of the building and light up, enjoying the taste of tobacco and battery acid and dishwashing detergent and whatever else it is they put in smokes.

I can hear the crunch of the guy's boots behind me as I round the corner and come to the back of the rest stop.

I keep walking until I am about twenty steps outside the circle of lights that surround the stop, but he still finds me. I stand there, smoking, my cigarette perched delicately between two fingers. I pretend I'm Audrey Hepburn in *Breakfast at Tiffany's*. Delicate. Demure. Helpless.

"Hey," the guy says. He's got a surprisingly high voice, not the gravelly rasp I was imagining. I turn to look at him. "Hey, you wanna have a good time?" he asks, his eyes shiny.

"No thanks," I say quietly. I always get real quiet in moments like this. My muscles are trembling, already flooded with anticipation and excitement.

"Aw, come on," he says, "I think we're gonna have a good time." And he wraps his big, meaty fingers around my wrist.

I jab the cigarette into his bare forearm. He yelps and lets me go. I rear back and bring my foot up, kicking hard in the Praying Mantis style. He hunches instinctively to protect his crotch, but I am aiming higher than that, and my kick catches him directly in his bottom left rib. I hear the bone crack, and the man wails in pain and surprise. The sound is musical to me, and I let out a whoop as I whip my fist up and around in a Leopard's Paw knuckle punch, breaking his nose and sending a spurt of blood into the air. A few drops hit my face, and I totally lose it then, abandoning myself to the dance of feet and fists until the man is curled up on the ground, at my mercy.

I pull myself back from the edge of animal fury just in time to stop myself from caving in his windpipe with my heel. I stand over his writhing body, breathing deeply. "You're right," I say to him, "that was a good time."

He whimpers and gargles, sounding like a choking kitten. I blow him a kiss over my shoulder as I'm walking away.

My father taught me how to kill a man with my bare hands. He was a martial arts expert back in the day, having grown up in an honest-to-god Shaolin temple and all, and he thought that punching and kicking stuff would make me a man. It didn't work out for him, but the skills have proven quite useful. When I was little, my dad used to drag me out into the backyard and make me punch an apple tree, over and over, for hours, till my knuckles split open. My blood went into the roots of that tree, and I swear this is why the apples always came out so red and so sweet in the fall.

from my notebook —

song of the pocket knife, part 2

my friend the small silver pocket knife
is someone I keep with me
always.
for comfort. and truth.
and protection.
not protection for myself
(my fists and feet
and elbows and knees
are already sharp enough
for that).
my friend the silver pocket knife
is for in case
i need to protect
someone from me.

Dear Charity,

Here's the letter I promised you, so you can stop worrying now, okay? And don't even pretend you weren't worrying about me. I'm the liar in this family, not you.

Anyway, just so you know, things have been fine with the trip so far. I slept on the bus the whole way here, and didn't even talk to anyone or get into any fights or anything. Pretty boring, to tell the truth. You always think that leaving home is going to be this huge terrifying adventure that shakes your soul to its very core and forces you to face the hidden depths of violence within, but mostly it's been listening to old mixtapes and staring at a lot of highway. So it goes.

The City has been pretty cool so far, you know, though I'm not sure it's as glam as everyone says it is. It's funny how every place is kind of two places at once: there's the glorious imaginary place made out of the dreams they sell in books, movies, and vacation package commercials, and then there's the real place, where people are commuting to work and taking shit from their bosses and going home to crap family lives just like everywhere else.

I'm thinking I'll get a job in a clothing or makeup

store or something, work for a year or three, and maybe register for a night class or something once I've got all this transition stuff worked out. See? Your crazy big sis can be responsible.

You probably don't remember this at all, but I actually used to be responsible all the time for a while there, just after you were born. Mom had to go back to work a couple weeks after, so I got to stay home and take care of you a bunch of the time, which was cool, because I got to miss school. You were the cutest, ugliest little raisin! And you used to cry, like, eighty percent of the time.

You had three different kinds of cries: One was like a constant whimpering drone that you used to tell people that you were awake. And then you had a kind of barking shriek that you made whenever you were hungry or had pooped yourself (aren't you glad you have an older sibling to remember all this for posterity, ha ha). And then you had this other cry, this kind of, like, wailing siren that sounded like a demented zombie housewife raising herself from the dead, and that one meant that you were sad or scared.

And whenever I heard that one, I would hold you and rock you and sing you the song. Remember? Mom used to sing it to me, but she stopped when she stopped singing period. It went like this:

> Whatever you dream of, I believe you can be
> From the stars in the sky to the fish in the sea
> Whether you walk or swim or crawl or fly high
> I'll always be here, I'll be near standing by
> And I will love, love, love you till the day that I die

And even beyond, little sis. I'll always be with you, no matter where I go.

Love,

Your sister

ps: I'm putting some pine needles in this envelope for your collection. Will send you an address so you can write back soon!

PART II: STREET OF MIRACLES

Fierce femmes

So the stories are true: the City of Smoke and Lights is full of fierce, fabulous femmes. Dangerous trans women, hot as blue stars. You can find them anywhere if you know how to look, and believe me, I am *looking*. Can't take my eyes off them: these visions of what I could be. What I am becoming.

My first trans woman friend found me the minute my feet touched the ground here. Her name is Kimaya, and she's *wonderful*. As I stood by the dingy bus station, blinking in the smoky air and gawking at all the people and cars swirling through the streets, she swooped down on me like a bejewelled bird out of paradise and said, "Are you lost, honey? *You* look like a girl who is going to get herself in trouble."

The fiercest and most powerful femmes in the City can be found on the Street of Miracles, located in the heart of downtown. Time is slow and memory fluid on the Street of Miracles, where it is always night. Here, anything at all can be lost, found, and purchased for the right price. Red-gold lanterns float on invisible strings between the rooftops of restaurants, theatres, bars, sex shops, lounges, strip clubs, hookah dens. Clouds of fragrant smoke waft through the air, which reverberates with thumping bass and people out to party.

Most of the folks you'll find on the Street come to play, here for an evening and back home by morning. This, however, is where the fierce femmes of the City live and work. It is their magic, more than anything else, that sustains the everlasting festival that the Street of Miracles is so well-known for.

Legend has it, my new friend Kimaya tells me, that the Street was created over seventy years ago, when a femme was beaten to death by a would-be john in front of a dozen bystanders. It was her spilled blood that brought about the perpetual nighttime. Her bones still lie somewhere beneath the cobblestones, along with her ossified heart, calling trans girls to her. Exhorting them to live their lives boldly, no matter the price. On the Street, she is a legend, a goddess.

They—we—call her the First Femme.

Already, in less than three weeks, I have met so many femmes. They are a pantheon of goddesses, each one unique:

There is Rapunzelle, Kimaya's lover, who is easily the most enormous person I have ever seen in my entire life. She blocks out the sun wherever she goes, an obsidian globe of a woman, always in boat-sized hot-pink leopard-print heels. Her weave is a forest of long gold braids, from which she derives her name. Rapunzelle always has something juicy to share—money she just made, food she just bought, gossip she just heard from the girls.

There is Lucretia, a white, blond princess with legs a mile long. Because she is gorgeous, she gets away with being nasty, and she revels in it.

There is Valaria, who is six feet tall with a shaved head. She always wears earrings made with a chain of spiked hoops and studded black leather boots. She rarely speaks, but when she does, her voice rolls like quiet thunder and everyone listens. To me, she looks like the Goddess of War.

There is Alzena the Witch, who is all bones and enormous golden eyes and long, painted fingernails. Alzena knows how to read the Tarot, cure a sore throat, put curses on people. She knows all about how to make someone fall in love with her, but not how to make them stop.

There is Esperanza, who speaks only Spanish and always wears bright red lipstick.

There is Marie-Eve, whose face is covered in wrinkles and is the only trans woman I have ever heard of who is over seventy years old.

There is Ivana.

There is Laurentine.

There is Soraya.

There is Gwen.

There is Ying.

There is Noor.

There is Morena.

And more, and more, and more, and more. Maybe more than I will ever meet.

And anything can happen now that I am here with them.

Kimaya's smile

Kimaya's smile is a slice of the yellow moon. It stands out against the darkness of her skin and reflects the light of her brandy-coloured eyes, which are large and crinkly at the corners from the hot sun of the island where she grew up and from so much smiling.

The smile is the first thing anyone notices about Kimaya because it is so bright and beautiful. Like the moon, it is ancient and battered and mysterious. Kimaya's smile is punctuated by several cracked teeth, each of which tells a story: some are from getting hit in the face by her boyfriend ten years ago, one is from a police baton during a protest, and some have been cracked for so long she can't remember how they got that way.

Kimaya's teeth stand out especially when she laughs, which is at least every few minutes. But there is nothing fake or forced about her smile. She is always genuinely happy to see you, to ask you what your name is and why you've come to the City of Smoke and Lights. She is truly delighted to show you the cheapest places to eat curry goat or Vietnamese noodles, to help you find an apartment where the rent is low and the landlords don't mind trannies. She says it's because she never had sisters to help her on her journey, and no one should have to go it alone.

She smiles even as she tells you this, but the smile is sad and full of unsaid things. Kimaya is only ten years older than me, but she has already seen and done so much more. She's worked in a fish-drying factory, studied at a university, travelled the world, become a dressmaker, and been married twice (once to a man and once to a woman), to name just a few. Sometimes I am jealous and sometimes I am grateful that I have not done as many things as her.

Kimaya's smile is a key: it opens doors to places that I desperately want and am afraid to go. It is a map, guiding the way. It is warm butter, melting on toast. It feels like sisterhood. It feels like open arms. It feels like home.

My own place

My little sister once came home from school when she was in the second grade and asked me, "What's a sanctuary?" I guess they had been reading about wildlife preservation or the Hunchback of Notre-Dame or something.

And it's funny because no one ever taught me this, and I can't even remember thinking about it very much, but the answer came flying right out of my mouth, like it had been waiting there since time immemorial.

"A sanctuary is a place where the door only locks from the inside." I looked her in the eyes as I said it, and I could see right away that she understood.

The crooked house where we grew up was like a giant spider web: the walls and floor trembled with every move you made, so that you could never be sure you were completely alone. And it stuck on you, grasped at you with its hungry windows and hungry doors, pulling you in so you couldn't leave, couldn't breathe, couldn't dream or achoo.

It ate you, that house. It kept you in it, but it didn't keep things out.

Now I live in a little tin box that someone decided to charge rent for. Kimaya helped me find it, the way she helps everyone find things that they're looking for, or that they've lost. It's at the top of the stairs of a crumbly building that overlooks an alley, across from which the Street of Miracles begins. The landlord is a guy with pale skin who wears a leather collar at all times.

"Even when I shower," he said, leering at me as he handed me the key. He seems nice enough, I guess.

The bed is a futon that takes up a third of the space. the other two thirds are filled up by a tiny wooden table, a mini-fridge with a hot plate on top of it, and a light bulb hanging from the ceiling. A fingernail slice of window looks out onto the alley.

I loved it with fierce, starving joy from the moment I stepped inside the place and the flimsy wooden door closed behind me. Loved it so much that I fell to my knees and stuffed my hand over my mouth and squealed as quietly as possible, then fell over onto my side and pummelled the futon with my feet and my fists like I wanted to kill it, like I wanted it to know how it hurt to love it so much.

Little tin box apartment, I know you aren't strong enough: not to keep me inside, nor to keep monsters out. But I don't care. You have a door that closes, and only I can lock it from the inside. You are a box of melting chocolates with my maraschino cherry heart squelching at its core. A pupa inside its shell.

Little cocoon apartment, I love how you rattle and shake in the wind. You are mine like nothing has ever been before. Someday you'll tear open, and I will fly out with the wings I have grown inside you. Still shimmering. Still wet.

The legendary romance of Kimaya and Rapunzelle

Rapunzelle comes over with a housewarming present: a baby orange tree that stands two feet tall in a little clay pot. Oranges the size of marbles are ripening on its branches, and it's so full of vibrant colour and life that it brightens the whole apartment.

"It's *perfect*," I say in awe, and Rapunzelle throws back her mane of glorious braids and squeals. "I got it from a flower shop in the *nice* part of town," she says proudly. "I looked at it and thought about you right away: a beautiful baby tree for a beautiful baby femme." And for a moment I can't speak because my throat's closed up and my eyes are stinging.

"Oh, baby," Rapunzelle says. "It's okay, now don't you worry about a thing. It's okay to cry." And I do, for the first time in forever; I sink into the soft, perfumed bulk of Rapunzelle's body and cry and cry and cry.

"Why are you being so nice to me, you and Kimaya?" I ask when I can finally talk again. "No one's this nice, not in real life."

She looks at me soberly. "You know, I used to think

that too," she says. "I used to have that look in my eye that you do now, the one where you've learned to hit things and hurt things and grab things because people have hit and hurt and grabbed you for as long as you can remember."

"I'm that transparent, huh," I say, and she laughs. It's like the ocean laughing, huge and dark, rolling waves full of life and salt and mysterious things.

"Honey, all the girls on the Street think they're so unique, but the truth is, we all come from the same story, more or less," she says.

"So what changed for you?" I ask.

"Kimaya," she says, after a moment of hesitation. "Kimaya changed things for me, like she does for all the girls. She's just like that: a special soul. It's her mission in life to make things better for us, and she does it one girl at a time, though I swear to god, I was probably the hardest case she ever had. Maybe that's why she and I are together now, because she had to work so hard to save me that she fell in love."

Absurdly, I feel a surge of jealousy. I can't help it. I thought I was Kimaya's special friend. But I push that thought right back down into the massive sludge pool of nasty thoughts at the bottom of my mind.

"How did you two meet?" I ask, and a grin breaks across her face.

"Well, let me tell you," she says, settling back. "That story's become a bit of a legend around here." And clearly one that she loves to tell. So I sit on the edge of my futon and let her tell it.

Rapunzelle was once a runaway, like me, but from the

way she tells it, she was running away from a hell of a lot worse. "Picture every possible terrible thing a father could do to his child," she says, eyes welling up with angry tears, "and then picture something worse. That's what my stepfather did to me."

So Rapunzelle came to the Street of Miracles, where she worked as a bartender at one of the clubs. But even beneath the gentle light and silk shadows cast by the lanterns of the Street, she couldn't let go of the terrible memories of her life before. "I hated myself," she says, "hated every last inch of this body that my dad had beaten so much poison into."

So she sought out drugs in order to forget: just weed at first, then speed, then harder and harder stuff. "There are some girls who can do drugs one day and then stop for a week or a month and then start up again whenever they want," she says, shaking her mane. "Good for them. I'm not one of those girls. I was hooked like a fish, right through the brain and the heart and the gut."

At the time, a vague number of years ago ("a lady never reveals her age," Rapunzelle opines), there was a powerful new drug that was flooding the market. "They called it Rapture in the rest of the City, but on the Street, we called it Lost," she says, her eyes going dreamy. "Because that's what it did to you when you took it, it made you lose everything you didn't like about the world. It changed you, not just on the inside, but on the outside too. Lost could give you blue eyes instead of brown, cat ears, a mermaid's tail, skin as green as an alien's, for as long as the high lasted. And when you were on it, you could be anything, anything at all except yourself."

Lost crept into Rapunzelle's veins, her nights, and then her days too, until she stopped going to work entirely. She spent all of her time on Lost, or thinking about Lost, or trying to scrape together enough money to get Lost. At the social support centre for trans women that Kimaya single-handedly founded and staffed, she got clean needles and tester kits, along with a good dose of advice from Kimaya: "Stop getting Lost and start thinking about how to solve the problems in her life." Rapunzelle promptly ignored these words, of course.

"All I wanted was to be on Lost forever," Rapunzelle stage whispers, staring off into space as though seeing herself through time. "And I lost everything: my job, my friends, my apartment. And the worst part was, I couldn't even feel anything about it. That's how completely, one hundred percent gone I was."

So Rapunzelle began to take bigger and bigger doses of Lost ("enough to change a mouse into an elephant," she says), until she became one of the most notorious addicts on the Street. "They all said I was out of control, but I knew exactly what I was doing," she says. "The only problem about being on Lost is that you always come back to yourself eventually. You always turn back into the thing you despise. I wanted to change *permanently*."

Then one night Rapunzelle went down to the club where she used to work to score some Lost, and, after shooting up in a bathroom stall, she saw something in the mirror that terrified her: her father's face. The horror of that vision sent her racing out onto the dance floor, where she began to change from one shape to another, faster and faster, until all that anyone could see when they looked at her was a blur—a shrieking, writhing, amorphous blur. All around her, people began to point and laugh at the wretched sight as the DJ continued to spin discs and bass pounded on and on.

Then a hush fell over the crowd. Someone had pulled the plug on the sound system. The only sounds were the crackling and squelching of Rapunzelle's flesh oozing as it transitioned from one shape to another—and the clack of a femme's high heels.

The throng of club goers parted like an enchanted sea. Through the path they made strode Kimaya, her face set in a mask of benevolent determination. Before her perfect posture and unrelenting gaze, the dancers flinched, ashamed of themselves. Ignoring them as she glided over the dance floor, majestic in four-inch heels and a green silk trench coat glimmering like a beetle's shell, Kimaya approached the whirlwind that Rapunzelle's body and soul had become. As she came within arm's reach, she paused for a moment.

And then she seized Rapunzelle in her embrace.

The Lost in Rapunzelle's system kicked into high gear at Kimaya's touch, flooding her mind with visions and memories. Rapunzelle howled in intensified agony as her body took on wilder and wilder forms: a kicking centaur, a giant worm, a hissing serpent with maggots for eyes, a swarm of stinging ants. Still, Kimaya held on.

A thicket of thorns, an electric eel, a pillar of salt, a column of flame.

Still, Kimaya held on.

A giant oak, a wave of sea water, a six-headed goat, a cloud of bats, a curtain of smoke.

Still, Kimaya held on.

A howling baby, a wizened crone, a rotting corpse, a weeping child.

Kimaya held on, and on, and on, until she was covered in bruises and burns and her own blood, until she was exhausted and on her knees, and still she held on—

until—

Rapunzelle was herself at last, once again.

"We fell to the floor, both of us," Rapunzelle says, tears flowing freely down her cheeks, "Totally exhausted. Everyone in the club was gone by this point. And I looked over at her and asked, *why did you hold on?* and she said—" Rapunzelle has to stop for a moment to recover her voice. Even after all this time and so many tellings, she is still choked up over this part of the story. I realize that I am holding my breath too. I reach out, grab Rapunzelle's hand, caught up in the surge of her feeling.

"She said to me, *because you're worth holding on to.*"

Boobs, or, Just as much as you

There is a run-down storefront on the Street of Miracles that is called the Femme Alliance Building, or FAB. Technically, it is a health and social services centre for trans women and sex workers. In reality, it is a severely underfunded three-room office where volunteers, directed by Kimaya, do their best to help trans girls get the things they need.

There isn't much in the way of furniture: a few beat-up sofas with the stuffing coming out of them and a ten-year-old computer that anyone can use. Yellowing posters for health clinics, legal rights workshops, political demonstrations, and cabaret shows cover the walls. But it's the femmes, not the furniture, that make the place fabulous: there are always at least three or four girls here, lounging in shimmering tights and heels, smoking indoors (ignoring Kimaya's scolding), and teasing each other. Sometimes they get into fights, which are vicious and last only a few seconds before they get broken up.

I am perched on the edge of a stained velvet couch that must have been gorgeous once, listening to the girls talk. I feel like a little moth next to extravagant butterflies. Except for Kimaya, no one pays any attention to me. I hate it, which surprises me, because back in Gloom, being ignored always made me feel safe.

Here in FAB, though, being ignored makes me feel small and invisible, makes me hate myself. I long to be a part of the conversations, to talk, to join the glittering flock.

I am pretending to look at a pamphlet on hormone therapy treatment when Lucretia the Princess swans into FAB. God, she's revolting, with her long white legs and perfect perky breasts and a mane of white-gold hair. She is always wearing expensive shoes bought by one of her rich boyfriends. This is how you know someone is cruel: they notice things no one else would notice so that they can make fun of them. Today, Lucretia notices me.

"Look, fresh meat!" she interrupts herself in the middle of a story about the fabulous hotel her latest boyfriend took her to. "Who's the kid?"

"That's Kimaya's new friend," says Laurentine. "She's from Gloom."

I am surprised she remembers.

Lucretia is up in my face now, sneering at me down her perfect little nose. "She doesn't even have boobs yet! How old are you, kid? Don't you wanna get boobs?" And she pokes my flat chest with her spiky nail.

Later, I will regret what happens next, even though lots of the girls will tell me Lucretia had it coming. I will wonder why I can never solve my problems with anything except violence. I will wonder how much of a problem this is.

I will wonder why I hurt people when what I really want is for them to love me.

Right now, though, it all happens too fast to think about: I am up off the couch, grabbing Lucretia's wrist. I twist up and over, spinning her around and slamming her face into the stained cushions. She lets out a muffled wail, and I grab her stupid blond hair with my free hand and yank her head up, pulling hard enough to let her know I mean business. The other girls shriek in surprise and delight. Nothing's better than a fight on a slow evening.

"Let's get one thing straight, you and I," I say, loud enough so everyone can hear. "I don't give a shit about how big your boobs are. I am just as much a woman as you." I look up, gazing around the room with eyes that say, *I'm as fierce and fabulous as anyone here, and I don't give a shit what you think.*

And I think everyone buys it except for me.

The waiting room

I have decided that I want boobs. There are many reasons for this and I don't have to justify them to anyone, Lucretia or otherwise. If I want to have boobs, take hormones, whatever, then that's my business and no one else's.

I asked Kimaya where I could get a doctor, and she told me to go to Dr. Crocodile's office on Razor Moon Avenue, a couple blocks away from the Street of Miracles. All the femmes go there to get their hormones done, Kimaya says, because Dr. Crocodile doesn't charge a fee.

"Although," she added, "he isn't doing it out of the goodness of his heart, you can be sure of that," and a cloud passed over her smile. I didn't ask for more explanation because I didn't want to know.

The waiting room of Dr. Crocodile's office is a big space on the fifteenth floor of a surprisingly fancy building for this area of town. The floor and walls are glaringly white, and reflect the harsh glow of the fluorescent light bulbs overhead. The chairs are also white and covered in clear thin plastic.

How can a room feel so dirty when it looks so clean?

There is a little white desk in the centre of the

room. The receptionist sits there. She is a middle-aged, tired-looking lady with cobalt blue skin. I walk up to her and explain why I'm here. She doesn't say anything, just stamps a card with a number on it, hands it to me, and waves at the chairs. I guess I'm supposed to sit, so I do.

It takes a while to find an empty chair. The room is filled with patients, all of whom look like they have been waiting for a long time. Like me, they are all here because they cannot afford to see another doctor. I can tell because of the way they smell, what they are wearing, what they look like. I don't mean that in a snobby way. After all, I am one of them.

There is a trio of teenage girls with light brown skin, tattoos, and hot-pink hair. They are all wearing revealing tank tops, combat boots, and cheap silver chains. Little insect wings flutter from their shoulders.

There is an old woman with ratty orange-striped fur and a tail. It looks like she once had a mouth full of fangs, but most of them have fallen out now.

There is a hairy man with goat horns and hooves. Blood flows slowly through a clear tube coming out of his arm and into a machine on wheels and then back into his veins.

There is a person who looks like a skeleton with skin tacked onto the bones as an afterthought. The only indication that they are alive is the shallow, rattling breaths coming in and out of their mouth.

There is a bald person who must have once had gigantic blackbird wings, but most of the feathers have fallen out. Some of them are falling out now, and they litter the bleached-bone-white floor like garbage.

I sit on the plastic-covered chair that is too clean for me, and I wait for what feels like hours, angry and sad. I am ashamed to be here, but I don't know why.

And looking into the dead marble eyes of the insect girls, the tiger lady, the bleeding goat man, the skin-covered skeleton, and the featherless angel, I can see that they are all ashamed as well.

We sit together and wait. For the time to pass. For the memories to fade. For the waiting to be over.

from my notebook —

song of the pocket knife, part 3

i love the blade
because it is honest,
because it is small and sharp like me,
because it hurts me with its love
instead of the other way around.

Dr. Crocodile

Dr. Crocodile is wearing a toothy grin when he reaches out to shake my hand. His palm is hot and moist, like a swamp. The grin never leaves his face, not once, the whole time we are talking.

"It's a pleasure to meet you," he says. "It's always a pleasure for me to help girls like you make their dreams come true."

"Oh," I say. "That's nice."

He leans in close, and his eyes are big and luminous. "So tell me about why you want to become a woman," he says.

"Well, I am already a woman," I say. "I just want, you know, breasts."

He nods, and the fluorescent light overhead reflects off his shining pale face. He has not blinked once. "Of course," he says, "of course. Well, I'll need you to undress for a thorough medical examination before I decide anything about your treatment options. It's all part of standard procedure. For your own safety, of course."

I was expecting something like this, but my muscles still clench up at the demand. An invisible ghostly hand lands on my shoulder, tugging gently but urgently, warning me away.

"Don't be shy, don't be shy," says Dr. Crocodile. "I won't bite, you know!"

I arrange my lips in a smiling shape. "Of course," I say. *Standard procedure. For your own safety, of course.*

I strip and get onto the examination table with its flimsy paper covering. The light bulb hangs directly above me, boring into my skin.

Dr. Crocodile snaps on a pair of black gloves and grins at me. "Wonderful," he says, "this shouldn't take but a moment."

There are many metal and plastic tools that Dr. Crocodile puts inside of me. He does not tell me why. He puts a long, shiny needle inside my arm and draws out seven small vials of blood. He touches me everywhere— long, lingering touches—with his rubbery gloves. He rolls me over and spreads my legs. He puts a little instrument up inside there and it scrapes some flesh out of my tender insides.

He does not blink once.

Angry killer bees swarm through my body, snarling and stinging. They boil beneath my nipples, inside my private parts. My arms and legs scream to get up, punch, kick, hurt. I could break Dr. Crocodile's toothy grin in half. I could snap his ribs and crush his windpipe. I could watch him bleed and beg for mercy. I do not move. I do not move.

Ghostly fingers brush my cheek.

"Well," says Dr. Crocodile, pulling off his gloves, "that wasn't so bad, was it?"

I say nothing, and put my clothes back on.

"I think you are going to make a very beautiful woman," he says to me. "You Asians are always the best treatment subjects for this sort of thing."

"Oh," I say.

"One last thing," he says, "before we start the treatment. We haven't discussed payment." His grin is oh so big.

"I was told that there was no charge at this clinic," I say, red-hot bubbles gurgling in my veins.

"Oh, of course, there's no monetary fee," he says. "That would be unconscionable. We're a non-profit organization, here."

"Well, then..."

"But there is something we do ask of all our patients. A little program we'd like you to participate in. All in the interest of science, of course," he says.

"I see," I reply. What else is there to say?

And he is eating me with his eyes, his unwavering smile, as he leans forward to whisper his price.

You know you're fish, right

You know you're fish, right?" Kimaya says as she stretch-es a sheet of red and gold fabric across her bed. She is go-ing to make me a dress out of it, though I don't know that I would ever wear any colour other than black. Or maybe grey. But it makes her happy to think about me swathed in one of her exquisite creations—that's what she calls them, "exquisite creations"—and making Kimaya happy is one of the simplest, nicest things I know how to do now that I live in the City of Smoke and Lights.

I think maybe I only know how to be kind to one per-son at a time. In Gloom, that person was my little sister. Here, it's Kimaya.

When Kimaya tells me that I am fish, I laugh out loud. *Fish* means that I am small and hairless with delicate bones. It means people will look at me and not know that I am a trans girl, that danger and lies and emptiness flow electric under my skin.

I laugh because while it is true that I am small and hairless and have a neat little face, I am also flat chested and have oily skin and thick hair that cannot be tamed. To me, *fish* means *beautiful*, means *glamorous*, means *doesn't look trans*. Like Lucretia or Alzena the Witch.

And I am not like them.

"Right," I say, "TOTALLY FISHHHH," and I vamp it up in front of the mirror, posing and pursing my lips like a model. Kimaya snorts and swats at me, and I flop down on the bed, giggling. Kimaya swats at me again as I land, crinkling up the fabric she is trying to measure.

"It's true, though," she says. "You, my dear, are a fishy, pretty girl. And you're smart. You could go far, you know."

"Ahhh, stop," I say, trying to laugh her off, but she won't let this go. She puts a hand on my arm, gentle but firm.

"You may not want to see it," she says, "but you were born to a certain privilege, dear."

A misty silence falls over us. I look at myself in the mirror again. Kimaya goes on, her voice tender but un-yielding.

"*Fish* means being able to walk in the daylight, as far as you please from the Street of Miracles, without fear of being chased and beat up by somebody or arrested by the cops. It means being able to get a job, one outside of selling the glamour and flesh men come looking to buy in secret in the night. It means maybe getting a boyfriend, sweet and handsome and uncomplicated, wealthy enough to take you to the highest towers of the City. That's what fish means, my dear ... and I want that for you."

I look at my reflection, and for the first time, I see that my hair, which I have always hated, is not just thick, but lush and shiny and starting to fall in waves past my chin. It frames my tilted eyes, which are almond shaped and long lashed, and my slanted cheekbones. The hint of breasts and hips are starting to grow over my bony frame. I see, for the first time, a pretty girl. Or a girl who will be pretty.

Kimaya is also looking in the mirror, and I meet her gaze there. There is a look I do not like in her expression, a hint of something that doesn't match her sweet tone and seems totally alien for my warm, generous femme sister. It is a look like I might wear—eyes narrow and lips pursed. She's peering at herself, not liking what she sees.

And I think about how *fish* means jealousy among femmes. About how we are all so hungry for what each other has, when the truth is none of us has enough to begin with. I think about how strange and funny it is that there are many femmes who would kill, who would sell their souls to Dr. Crocodile, for the chance to leave the Street of Miracles, when all my life I have been running toward it.

And I think about how Kimaya is right, how *fish* means opportunity and privilege. Someday, I may swim away from here into another place. I remember my little sister back in Gloom, and how escaping always seems to mean leaving someone behind.

Ghost hands run over my hair.

Kimaya stands up and puts herself between me and the mirror. She takes my hands in hers.

"Come on, fishy girl," she says, "I have to measure you for this dress."

Heels

My first pair of heels are a dark shiny luscious red that makes them look molten, like crimson liquid in a shoe-shaped mould. I found them at Lilith's Den, a thrift store run by the grey-haired femme named Marie-Eve. She is by far the oldest trans lady that anyone in the City knows, but she never tells anyone her actual age. Her crumpled-paper face crinkles up even more than normal when she sees me dig them out of a huge bin of discarded footwear.

"YES, GIRL! YOU'VE FOUND TREASURE THERE!" she bellows so loudly that all the other customers flinch and duck as the wobbly, floor-to-ceiling piles of vintage clothing threaten to crush us all. But Marie-Eve has lived too long to give a shit about what anyone thinks, so she just comes out from behind the counter toward me to chortle like a happy, sequin-bedecked walrus about how lucky I am to have found these shoes.

"A femme's heels are her armour, girl," she tells me with the air of a veteran war hero imparting the secret of valour to a new trainee. "The right pair of shoes makes you unstoppable."

I don't need her to tell me twice. The shoes are red as lollipops, red as adventure, red as my crazy violent blood, and they want me to put them on, right now. So I do, and Marie-Eve gives them to me for the grand total of one dollar, which makes all the other customers grumble, but they shut up real quick when Marie-Eve gives them the stink eye.

And then I am out on the Street in my shiny red shoes, with their high high heels, and I feel like I am walking on a desert wind, fast and powerful enough to strip the flesh from a skeleton. My legs are longer than I am used to, and my calves look like a different person's. I feel lean and strong and sexy, like a secret agent superspy assassin femme fatale. Taller in my heels, I am closer to some dangerous heaven.

The shoes are even more powerful than I bargained for. They make my hips sway and dance, and they lengthen my spine, making people stop and glance for longer than they should. The way they look at Kimaya or Lucretia or even tall Valaria the Goddess of War.

There is admiration and jealousy and desire and fear and hatred in those looks, all in the space of a few seconds, and the combination makes my head spin. Every so often men will whistle at me, or holler a disgusting invitation or a threat to pound my faggot face into the pavement. I want to lash out at them, to break their bones like my father taught me to, but the shoes whirl me away, so fast and so confident that I do not have time to get into fights.

When I get home to my tiny tin box apartment, I take the shoes off and collapse onto the futon. My heart is pounding and my head hurts worse than a hangover. Something inside me is different now, though I couldn't tell you what it was. All I know is, a femme's heels are serious business.

The story of Soraya

Soraya is dead. Her body was found yesterday in a dumpster behind a hotel on Scarlet Avenue, just one block from the Street of Miracles. Rumour has it she was beaten to death with a bottle, because tiny shards of glass were found embedded in her scalp and cracked skull. The police are refusing to release many details but have announced to one news source that cares that they have not yet ruled it a homicide. As if she might have happened to have fallen headfirst onto a bottle, oh, seventeen times or so. They will not investigate further—why should they? A trans girl is found dead at least once every year in this city.

I can hear some of their names filtering through the murmur of the crowd: *Marilene. Lotte. Ilsa.* Names of women I never knew but feel connected to, in some terrible way.

The news sends a ripple of anger and grief through the trans femmes of the City of Smoke and Lights. We gather in groups of five, ten, even twenty, cramming glamorous bodies into the tiny Femme Alliance Building. Orange sparks fly through the air wherever our shoulders rub together.

"We can't just let the city bury this," says Rapunzelle,

shaking her braids. "We have to stick together, femmes. We have to push back!" The other girls murmur and nod in agreement.

"What can we do?" Lucretia asks. "The police won't do anything. We're nothing to them, remember? They couldn't care less if we live or die." For once, I agree with her.

"We have to get into the streets," Rapunzelle says. Her face is feverish, and Kimaya puts a hand on her back, steadying her. "We have to demonstrate," Rapunzelle continues, "show the mayor that we won't just sit quietly waiting for someone to kill us, too. Even if we have to go right into his backyard and yell it into his bedroom."

Valaria stands up, tall and imposing. Her bare scalp gleams like the moon. "The mayor?" she asks scornfully. "The mayor and his pigs have always worked against us, not for us. Everyone knows that. If we want justice for Soraya, we'll have to take it ourselves."

There is more murmuring among the girls:

"It will only hurt more to fight a battle that has already been lost," intones Alzena the Witch, from a shadowy corner. "Avenging Soraya won't bring her back. This is the Street of Miracles—it was created when the First Femme sacrificed herself, and when one of us dies, we continue her legacy. Soraya was killed so that the rest of us could live."

"I still think that we should go to City Hall," Rapunzelle begins to say, but she is interrupted by the other girls, all of whom are shouting now, trying to get heard. The conversation becomes more and more frenzied, as though the spirit of Soraya is whirling faster and faster among us, a tornado of fury and terror.

Dizzy, I slip out the door and into the lantern-lit Street. The air outside is perfumed as always, the light soft and the shadows intoxicating. Packs of people stroll by, laughing and talking and pawing at each other like animals in heat. Lust covers them like an iridescent film.

I glance through the door of a club where huge men with oiled muscles are dancing onstage. More men wearing the suits and ties of the business class of the City of Smoke and Lights are watching and clapping and throwing money into the air.

I look down a set of stairs into another club, a basement, where people are dancing in costumes and masks and waving glowing amulets in the air. They are dressed as demons, princesses, punk rockers, mermaids, witches, leather daddies, schoolgirls in short skirts. Not one of them knows the story of Soraya, or even her name.

I remember Alzena the Witch's words: *Soraya died so the rest of us could live.*

Could that be true? People come to the Street of Miracles to forget their sorrows, but we come here to give up our memories, our bodies, our whole selves. Trans girls flow through the Street like blood in an artery, feeding the illusions, the miracles that everyone is so hungry for.

Does the Street shelter or sacrifice us? And what's the difference?

Luminous green moths flutter around me, poetry whispering from their extravagantly tailed wings. I think of Soraya.

I never got a chance to know her, really. I got here too late, she died too soon. She was a girl with light brown skin who wore calf-length boots and gorgeous huge wings of green eyeshadow. She was quiet, smiled shyly at me whenever we ran into one another. I don't know if I would ever have spoken to her, if I would have cared enough to think about her half as much when she was alive as I do now that she is dead. Now that I can see my own body imprinted over the mental image of her corpse.

Soraya's story. Why didn't I ask her before it was too late? Why wasn't I more curious, more interested, less self-absorbed? Do any of the girls on the Street know Soraya's story? Or is it lost to me, lost to us all now?

How many stories of trans girls have been lost here?

Soraya's story. I invent the details to the sound of the moths' wingbeats: She was born in a city far from here, to immigrant parents a little like mine. They were a professor of literature and an engineer back in the old country, but by the time Soraya was born, they ran a tiny corner store in the middle of town that sold kebabs and lentil rice with lamb and egg yolks alongside the cigarettes and beer. They taught Soraya to pray every day of her life, and she never missed a single one, even when she came to this city where no one believes in God anymore.

Every day, Soraya prayed that her family would still love her, even though she had left them and their hopes for her education to become a dancer in a bar where strange men whooped and hollered at her and, later in the evening, paid her three hundred dollars for a full body massage. Perhaps because she prayed, her family never stopped. Her father phoned her every Saturday afternoon, and they spoke for hours, long-distance charges be damned. Her mother sent her care packages of lentil rice with lamb and egg yolks, and just the scent of saffron rising from the open container was enough to make Soraya weep.

She liked fancy chocolates and was good at math. She wanted to be a fashion photographer someday. She was twenty-seven years old when, during a slow month at the bar, she ignored her better judgement to say yes to a man who offered her seven hundred dollars to come with him to a sketchy hotel instead of staying in one of the backrooms at the bar.

Soraya considered herself lucky. With seven hundred dollars, she could make rent after all, put a few dollars away for her camera fund, send a gift to her mother. In her final moments, as he beat her to death, Soraya closed her eyes and prayed. This time, she asked God if He could see to it that her parents loved her a little less so as to not mourn her too much. She did not want them to suffer in their old age.

As Soraya exhaled her final breath, a cloud of luminous green moths with eye-shaped patterns on their wings fluttered out of her mouth and nose. They hovered above the dumpster where her body had been abandoned, and then flew up and away, carrying the remainder of her spirit to the Street of Miracles, where sweaty college boys were grinding their hips against each other and men threw money into the air as they temporarily forgot their wives.

Feeling free at last from the burden of their everyday lives, the revellers of the endless party raised their arms toward the moon as the moths darted about, searching for someone to receive their story. No one slowed down, however, to listen to the whispering of their wings, or to remember Soraya's name. Not a single lantern was extinguished, no one stopped for even a moment. She was not the first trans girl to die here praying to God and thinking of home, and she would certainly not be the last.

Girl gang

That day, after we learn that Soraya was murdered, Valaria the Goddess of War finally declares that enough is enough: too many femmes have died in the City with no one seeking justice. "It's time to fight back," she says to the group of us on the sidewalk outside the Femme Alliance Building. She looks each of us in the eye. "Who's with me?"

Whispers sweep through the knot of femmes. Some look eager, others afraid. Everyone is buzzing with nervous energy.

"We don't know how to fight," says Noor, shaking her magnificent mane of dark red extensions. The plastic beads of her many waist-long necklaces clatter in agreement. "What do you want us to do, exactly? Go out there and start bashing the straights? Some of us actually like straight boys, you know, and more importantly, a lot of us make our cash from them. Not every femme is *you*, Valaria."

I'm impressed. I would never talk like that to the Goddess of War.

"Trans girls fight every single day of our lives," Valaria says, crossing her bare arms. The curves of her muscles shine in the light of the Street's lanterns, a call to battle. "We are always in danger, no matter where we go," she continues. "Whether we fight back or not, someone will always be trying to kill us. The question is, what are we going to do about it? Cower and wait for them to keep on picking us off one by one? Or make them more afraid of us than we are of them?"

Kimaya speaks then, a dark silhouette in the rectangle of light cast by the FAB doorway. "Girls of the Street," she says, and her voice is as strong, in its own way, as Valaria's. "I hear that you are angry. I hear that you are scared. But we cannot afford to stoop to the level of our oppressors: for one thing, violence only begets violence. We are better than that. We are *stronger* than that," she adds, casting a look in Valaria's direction. "Soraya's death is a tragedy and injustice, and not the first. I, of all people, know that. How many years have I spent on the Street of Miracles? How many girls have I seen lost to the ugly things that happen here? Now is the time to gather around each other and give each other love. There will be a place and time to bring about justice for Soraya, and I guarantee you that we will get to that place and time only with love. Not violence."

Several of the girls mhmm and nod in agreement. Laurentine actually applauds and says, "Thank you, Kimaya, for your wisdom." Noor echoes her, sharply.

Kimaya nods graciously, a queen receiving her dues. She looks over to where Rapunzelle and I are standing next to each other. Instinctively, I open my mouth to agree with her. But before I can, I sense a shiver going through Rapunzelle's body that stops me from speaking. I look over at her, and can see the pain in her eyes. She's torn, I realize, between Valaria's vision and Kimaya's. And now that I think of it, so am I. I grab Rapunzelle's hand, and she squeezes mine in return.

Hurt flickers through Kimaya's face. For a moment, her confidence falters, and Valaria senses it, taking advantage of the moment to speak up again.

"Kimaya," she says, her voice a low, dangerous purr. "No one here can question your wisdom or experience. The Femme Alliance was built on the back of your hard work, and for fifteen years, you've helped so many of us to survive. But times are changing. *We* are changing. Some us want more than survival, want more than hiding in the shadows and barely scraping by, kowtowing to the police and to any man who decides that the Street of Miracles is *his* home more than ours.

"It's all good to talk about love, but love didn't save Soraya. And it didn't save Irena before her, or Gwenivere, or Arianna, or Marilene, or Shelline. It didn't save Lune, or Lotte, or Ilsa." As she intones the names of these girls who have died before I got to the Street, ghost nails rake over my skin.

Kimaya flinches, as if punched. When she speaks again, her voice is shaky. "There is a way to fight without violence—" she begins to say.

"By writing letters to the government? Offering *sensitivity workshops* to the police?" Valaria spits out the words like they mean something dirty. "If those things worked, they would have worked fifteen years ago when you first opened FAB.

"It's time to fight back for real," she says, turning

away from Kimaya to appeal to the crowd. "It's time to make them *afraid* of us, for once, instead of the other way around. It's time to make any man think twice before he decides to rob us, beat us, hurt us. And let me tell you, there is only one way to do that."

There is a moment of silence. Then, chaos reigns. Kimaya raises her arms, trying to regain control, but the tide has turned, and Valaria's grin is full of knives. Rapunzelle's grip on my hand grinds the bones together.

To my surprise, it's Lucretia who steps forward to claim the floor next. "Valaria is right," she says. Her blond hair stands out starkly against the dark sky. "We have to take the fight to them."

And then my own mouth is speaking for me, before I can consciously decide to. "I'm in," I say, and my body thrills in reply. "I know how to fight."

Lucretia snorts and shoots me a poisonous look. "Of course *you're* in, you little psycho," she mutters under her breath. I pretend not to hear it.

"I'm in," says Kiki.

"Yes, yes!" says Esperanza enthusiastically. Lucretia turns to her and scoffs. "You don't even know what we're talking about," she says, enunciating loudly and slowly, as though to a very young child.

Esperanza turns to face Lucretia and, with icy deliberateness, takes a step to close the distance between them. Then she raises her left palm and her right fist to the level of her eyes and slams them together.

There's not a doubt in anyone's mind that she understands.

"Me too," says Ying.

"Me too," says Ivana.

"You bitches are suicidal," Noor says, stamping her heel. "Do what you want. I'm not going to go around getting busted up and fucked over by the cops. I'm as torn up as any of you that Soraya's gone, but she wouldn't have wanted anyone else to die over it." And she walks away. Morena and Laurentine hesitate, then follow suit, murmuring their agreement. Alzena the Witch says nothing, just melts into the shadows.

Now only Rapunzelle and Kimaya have yet to speak. Slowly, Rapunzelle approaches the doorway of the Femme Alliance Building, looking into her lover's eyes. Kimaya grips Rapunzelle's wrist, knuckles turning pale. A silent tension builds and builds between them. Kimaya shakes her head. Rapunzelle flinches, then pulls away.

"I'm sorry, baby," Rapunzelle says, "but Valaria is right. If femmes are going to keep dying anyway, then I want to say that I at least tried to do something about it." And she steps out of the doorway's rectangle of light and comes to stand beside us.

Kimaya stands completely still. I don't think she's even breathing. She looks as though she's been struck by lightning. And I know that a part of her will never forgive this betrayal, not from Rapunzelle, not from me. For a second, I am afraid that she won't survive it.

But then the grace and poise that she has developed over a lifetime of survival and leadership flows back into her veins. She takes a deep breath. Steadies herself against the doorframe of FAB.

"Go, then," she says, and her voice is bitter but gentle. "If that's what you have to do."

She looks so fierce and so fragile, standing there alone in the light cast by this tiny community centre—this haven, this shrine she has built and maintained by herself for all these years. I want to go to her, comfort her. But it's not me she wants.

Valaria nods, the new queen accepting her victory. "Thanks for everything you do, Kimaya," she says. But Kimaya has already turned away, leaving the door of FAB open. The rest of us stand in a semicircle on the Street of Miracles, waiting for Valaria to lead us into battle.

And just like that, our girl gang is formed.

Dear Charity,

First of all, thanks for writing. Second, YOU'RE
GETTING INTO FIGHTS AT SCHOOL NOW??? I don't
care what that white girl said about your shoes,
you can't be just sucker punching people all over
the place. Or have you forgotten about the sixty-
three times I got suspended? You care too much
about school for that. Kid, this is so not your lane.
I'm the delinquent one, remember??

Seriously, I know that this is going to sound
hypocritical, but look, Charity: you don't want to
be me. Once you start hurting people, you can't
stop.

Let me tell you something that I haven't told
you before: I've always been the fighter so you
didn't have to. Remember when you were five
and broke Dad's TV because you wouldn't stop
running around the house and tripped on the
cord? It was a shitty, tiny black-and-white TV
that only got three channels but it was the only
one we could afford. And Dad came out of the
bedroom and he was going to spank you with the
long wooden back-scratcher.

I used to let him spank me all the time, even
after I got big enough and good enough at kung
fu to make him stop, but when he went to hit

you, something inside me broke, you know? And I caught that back-scratcher in my hands as he brought it up for the first blow, and I pulled it away and broke it in half.

He spun to look at me, and we just stood there staring at each other for a long, terrifying moment.

Then I said, "Try that again and I'll kill you, Dad." Real calm. And that was it. We never talked about it again, but he also never really loved me after that.

When you fight back, when you hurt people, it makes them stop loving you, Charity. I don't want that for you.

Sincerely,

Your sister

ps: Oh yeah, as for me, everything's fine here. Have been working at a grocery store and going to a french class at night. Je suis tres bonne au francais maintien! Everything is great, nothing to worry about, definitely no violence or murders or anything.

pps: Sending a pack of real, live City cigarettes for your collection like you asked (NOT FOR YOU TO SMOKE).

PART III: GIRL GANG

The legend of the Lipstick Lacerators

For once, the City lives in fear of us. We are creatures out of a suburban businessman's nightmare: Fierce femmes on a mission of vengeance. Trans girls out for blood. With rhinestoned brass knuckles and spike heels, we hit the streets and the men who think they own them.

And girl, is it *so fun*.

It begins in the alley behind the dirtbag hotel on Scarlet Avenue, where Soraya was murdered and her body dumped like a piece of trash. We wait for the first rich-looking suit-and-tie type in a rumpled coat to stumble out the back door—and we pounce.

Valaria is the first, coming in fast and hard from the front. The guy barely has time to look up before her gloved fist hits his gut. I almost feel sorry for him. He doubles over, wheezing, and I move from the side, dropping into a sweeping kick that takes his legs out from under him. He hits the ground like a bag of cement, and the other girls lunge forward for the takedown. It's all over in a few seconds, and then the guy is unconscious but breathing, lighter one wallet with eighty dollars in it and a pair of leather wingtip shoes.

Before we leave, Ivana pulls a can of spray paint out of her denim jacket. "Gotta leave a souvenir," she says, smiling wickedly. And she tags the alley wall with the stain left by a lipstick kiss. Over that, she writes in huge, looping cursive:

YOU MESS WITH FEMMES YOU MESS WITH US

And we all shriek and applaud and then we are run, run, running away into the endless night.

Things are a blur after that. We become better at hunting, less sloppy and more thoughtful: Ying points out that we can't keep hitting places where trans girls work, because we'll scare the clients away, even the good ones.

So instead, we stalk the downtown core, in and around the Street of Miracles. Our targets are men, but not just any men: not the ones who work on the Street, the ones who are homeless, the ones who are known to be regulars and don't give anyone any trouble. We go for college boys, businessmen, tourists, nasty types who come here looking for a thrill.

Sometimes, a femme will tip us off about a mean manager at work or a bad client or a landlord trying to screw her over, and we make a special plan for him. Sometimes, we set a trap by sending one of us as bait to lure out assholes who like to pick on trans girls.

But most of the time, we stalk our prey, searching for the ones who are alone or who straggle, breaking away from the packs of men that swagger through downtown, boisterously obnoxious and unafraid. We follow them into alleyways, parking lots, dark corners. There is no shortage of secluded places in the City of Smoke and Lights—places where so many femmes have been beaten and died alone.

This time, we are the hunters. A pride of lionesses on the prowl. Dressed in black and extravagant bedazzled dollar-store masks, we ride the perfumed winds.

We take cash, credit cards, watches and jackets, cell phones and laptops. We leave bruises and fractured bones in our wake. All's fair in the war for survival, right? We split rich-boy skin over our knuckles, stomp creepy-dude ass all over the pavement. Rapunzelle has the idea that we should hit businesses too, places on the Street where trans girls aren't allowed to go, so we break some restaurant windows and slit the owners' car tires. Everywhere we strike, we leave our tag: a pair of golden lips.

"We're sending the City a message," says Valaria, flushed with sweat and adrenaline. "We're here. We're dangerous. Don't fuck with femmes."

And at last, the City seems to see us in its fear. We are in headline after headline. We are the talk of the town:

TRANSSEXUAL MENACE COMES TO TOWN.

TRANSGENDER TERRORISM?

PLEASURE SEEKERS BEATEN IN PLEASURE DISTRICT, MUGGED BY VIGILANTE GIRL GANG.

My personal favourite is:

LIPSTICK LACERATORS STRIKE TERROR ON THE STREET OF MIRACLES.

On the uses of elbows and knees

It doesn't take long before the men of the City decide to retaliate against the Lipstick Lacerators. As Rapunzelle puts it, "No one's gonna take kindly to a bunch of trannies running around beating up cis dudes."

Valaria, Rapunzelle, and I have been teaching the other girls how to fight properly. While I've had the most formal martial arts training, Valaria has the most experience. She moves with the look of someone who's been in dozens, maybe hundreds, of fights and won them all. When Valaria fights, her gaze is cool and steady. She does it because she has to, because she believes in what she's fighting for.

She doesn't love it the way I do.

Rapunzelle is a dirty fighter. She uses chains, a tire iron, her nails, whatever's available. She learned how to fight growing up in a town far to the south, she says, where she had to be constantly on guard against attack—at school, at work, at home where her drunken stepfather was the most dangerous enemy of all. She teaches the girls about survival, as much as Valaria teaches us about justice.

And me? I teach the skills my father taught me: Where to put a fist to inflict maximum damage, as quickly as possible, on another human. How to play to your body's strengths and opponent's weaknesses. The uses of elbows and knees. How to hurt someone. That's what I know best.

No amount of training is enough, though, to really prepare us for the night of our first real fight.

I saw a musical once, put on at my high school, about two rival gangs and one person from each fell in love with the other. There was a song and dance routine about a gang fight, which they called a "rumble." The actors danced with these side-stepping, slinky movements and snapped their fingers in unison.

This isn't really like that.

We run into the group of men carrying baseball bats and pool cues in a park at the end of the Street of Miracles. They spot us, a group of femmes wearing our bejewelled masks, and it's immediately clear that they have been hunting us, just like we have been hunting them.

There are maybe ten or twelve of them, all big guys with gorilla fists and mean faces. A dozen of them to the seven of us femmes.

"Two of them to one of us, and still *we* got *them* outnumbered, girls," says Valaria, stepping forward. Her voice rings out across the park.

One of the men, the biggest and nastiest looking, sneers, "We're gonna fuck you up good, ya buncha faggots. How about we cut your dicks off for ya?"

"Please," says Rapunzelle, "one of us has got more balls than all of you combined."

As one, the men roar and charge us. The world dissolves into a swirl of fists, feet, and flying teeth in the moonlight.

One of them rushes me, baseball bat upraised, and I take him out cleanly, with a huge, arcing punch to the face that snaps his head back and sends a lightning bolt of pain through the bones in my hand, wrist, and arm.

The pain sends me into an instant frenzy, and I snatch up the bat and slash it through the air at the next man. It bounces off his collarbone with a cracking sound, and he howls and falls to his knees. I kick him in the nose, feel it cave under the sole of my shoe. He screams again and grabs my ankle, twisting it, and I go down on my back. Instantly another man drops down, straddling me and pinning my wrists with one hand, choking me with the other.

I struggle to breathe and the whole world slows down.

All around me, the other femmes are locked in combat. Valaria has the leader guy in an armlock and is repeatedly slamming his head into a tree—

—Ivana jumps on a barrel-chested bald man's back, clawing at his eyes, and he grabs her arms and flips her over his head so that she hits the ground. I can hear the sound of her bones snapping. Ying wails and rams the guy—

—Esperanza screams as one of them drags her down by the hair, punching her repeatedly in the gut—

—we're losing we're losing and I can't breathe no air no air as the edges of my vision go fuzzy grey and the man on top of me bucks and brays in triumph, his hips grinding mine and bees bees killer bees flooding my veins—

—and then Valaria lets out a long, ululating war cry

that pierces the greying fabric of my consciousness and cracks the night in half. In her voice I hear the howling of coyotes and the roaring of an insect swarm, echoing through ancient forests and rivers rushing to carve through mountain canyons. And beneath that, the voice of a woman, violated and enraged—

—and for just a moment, as my lungs scream and my ears ring with Valaria's cry, the full moon seems to transform, to take on the shape of a face of a luminescent woman with rounded cheeks and full lips under long-lashed closed eyes and masses of curly hair. Her eyes open, and she whispers, "Live."

—and with a strength that comes from somewhere outside myself, I tear my left hand free and seize the ear of the man who's choking me.

And *pull*.

He recoils instantly, releasing my throat to press his hand to the shredded shell of his ear. Sweet oxygen floods my lungs, and I suck it in greedily, then grab his hair and pull his head toward mine, bringing up my forehead as I do so to break his nose. I push him aside and roll to my feet.

Rapunzelle body slams the man who's got Esperanza by the hair, then grabs around his neck and uses him as a battering ram to knock another opponent off his feet. Ivana has risen, one arm hanging at an unnatural angle, and she and Ying are furiously kicking the man who took her down.

Kiki is knocked to the ground by a roundhouse punch, and I rush forward to save her but to my surprise, Lucretia is already there, holding a piece of chain in her hand.

In a single swift movement, she loops it around the man's neck and pulls it tight, yanking him to the ground. As he falls, she knees him in the stomach, then kicks him in the head. Her full lips are drawn back in a snarl, and there is a crazy light in her eyes that I know very, very well. Behind her, Valaria dances and twirls, throwing out punches and kicks like the pain-inflicting goddess that she is.

The tide is turning, and we femmes catch on fire. We hurl ourselves into the fight with renewed rage, all the years of being harassed and insulted and threatened and beaten and watching sisters die one after another igniting to explode in our jackhammer fists and hearts.

And then, as suddenly as the fight began, it is over, the men hobbling and crawling to get away, dragging bloodied comrades with them. A few call out curses and threats as they retreat, and we hasten them along, throwing stones and broken bottles in their wake.

The enemy vanquished, we come together, a circle of femmes, checking the status of each other's injuries. There are bruises and shallow wounds, probably several fractured bones. But we are all standing. All still alive. Valaria raises her arms and howls in victory, and the rest of us do the same, intoxicated by our own power and violence. None of us has ever felt anything like this, regardless of how long we have spent living on the Street of Miracles. Nothing has prepared us to feel this connected to one another, to feel this strong.

Above us, a red ring glows around the moon.

The legend of Valaria the Goddess of War

A few hours after the fight, we are lying in a pile on the floor of the abandoned warehouse in the old Factory District that has become the unofficial base of the Lipstick Lacerators. Through the cracks in the ceiling, we watch the stars fade as the sky grows lighter. The whole gang is here except for Ivana, whose ribs might have been cracked in the fight, and Valaria, who's taken her to see Alzena the Witch instead of the hospital.

"We can't trust those people," Valaria insisted, though none of us had actually raised any objection. "Hospitals weren't made for girls like us. Alzena will fix her up just fine." Ivana smiled weakly and nodded at us as they left.

We're all exhausted and sweaty, and our clothes are stained with blood, but no one seems to want to go home, or to sleep, because we keep on talking—about clothes, about where we've come from, about dates. I've never felt so close to a group of women, or to anyone, really.

I also never thought that my ability to fight would bring me close to anyone. A part of me knows this can't possibly last—that sooner or later, they'll find out what

I'm really like, and stop being my friends. But until then, all I can do is try to enjoy this moment.

As we lie in the warm arms of the night, a thought occurs to me.

"So what's Valaria's story?" I ask. A wave of soft laughter breaks over the femmes.

"You mean you haven't heard it yet?" Lucretia asks scornfully. "I thought everyone had heard that old piece of gossip by now."

Leave it to Lucretia the Long-Legged Bitch to ruin my moment of sisterly connection. I open my mouth for a sharp retort, but before I can get the words out, Rapunzelle breaks in.

"Ahhh, stop it, Lucretia. She's still new, remember? Anyway, it's a good story." Rapunzelle reaches over to grab my hand and, in true Rapunzelle style, launches into the tale. As she does, the other femmes jump in, taking over and adding to the narrative so that Valaria's past is handed to me in a tapestry woven with femmes' voices.

According to the legend, Rapunzelle tells me, Valaria the Goddess of War was once the most celebrated drag queen on the Street of Miracles. By day, she worked as a hairdresser to rich women in the City under the name of Darren, but by night, she threw off her drab colours and set the stage ablaze as the Duchess Gloriana Cochrain with her hilarious, sexy impersonations of famous divas said to be even fiercer and more awe-inspiring than the original acts.

Among all the denizens and frequenters of the Street, the Duchess was known for her massive collection of wigs, each of them painstakingly curated and meticulously maintained, in over a thousand hairstyles, from the contemporary to classic to archaic to space-age edgy. According to those who knew her at the time, Ying adds, the Duchess never wore a coiffure twice, and she took pride in outstripping all the other performers in the district with her glamour.

Yet for all her admirers—and there were many—the Duchess never took a lover for either affection or money, out of deference to her boyfriend, a sweet man from a farm outside the City whose name none of the girls on the Street can remember anymore. You see, this man wasn't hard or grasping or jealous or rich, like most of the men they knew. He had a gentleness about him, Rapunzelle recalls, a tenderness so subtle that he became almost invisible as he followed the Duchess everywhere, shadow-like, a faithful moon in the orbit of her beauty—though to those few who cared to watch, he shone with adoration as he watched the Duchess pose and pout onstage.

No one knows, Ying whispers, how this man and the Duchess met, nor how long they had been together—only that their love was sacrosanct, a rock-solid constant on the ever-changing landscape of intrigue and lovers' betrayals on the Street of Miracles.

One night, after a performance comprising twenty-one solo numbers, each featuring a different outfit, the Duchess and her boyfriend slipped out the back door of the club where she had just received a standing ovation and dozens of roses thrown from feverish hands onto the stage. Normally, the Duchess changed back into her "civilian clothes," as she called them, before going home from a performance, but she was desperate to avoid the clinging men who stalked her constantly, begging for her affection. Earlier that morning, she had decided that this show would be her last: she would end her stage career with a bang, and then give up both her drag and daytime personas in order to usher a new woman into the world.

So she took her gentle boyfriend's hand and they ran together through the alleyway, drunk on music and booze and applause.

What happened next, Lucretia murmurs, no one knows for certain: It was one of the Duchess's spurned admirers, some say, egged on by drunken friends; others swear that it was a rival drag queen driven mad by jealousy. Still others insist, perhaps most realistically, that it was nothing but a chance run-in with a group of angry men looking for trouble, like so much of the violence that happens on the Street every night.

Whatever happened, the facts are these, Rapunzelle declares: Valaria's boyfriend was killed that night, his lung punctured by the jagged edge of a broken bottle and several other organs ruptured by blunt force trauma. He lay in the alleyway for over an hour before the ambulance finally arrived, while the Duchess Gloriana Cochrain, reigning drag queen of the Street of Miracles, held him in her arms, sobbing, his blood soaking every inch of her waist-length wig.

In the small hours of that morning, the Duchess burst unannounced into Alzena the Witch's house (Ying and Kiki were there, getting their Tarot cards read), blood-encrusted wig askew, makeup running so that it looked like a demon's mask. Without saying a word, Alzena the Witch rose from her rocking chair and ushered the

Duchess into her bedroom, closing the door behind her. Try as they might, Ying and Kiki could only make out a word or two of what was said, though they're sure that some kind of terrible magic was made that night, that the Duchess sold her soul or some other precious part of herself in return for the chance to speak with her lover's ghost, or perhaps for invincibility in battle, or maybe just for relief from the pain of her sorrow.

The next part of the story is the stuff of myth: The Duchess went home and stripped off her coiffure and gown and washed off her face. Then she picked up the blood-soaked wig and threw it in a plastic garbage bag, followed by all the rest of her wigs. She doused the luscious, shimmering tangle of locks in hairspray, and set them on fire in a metal trash can on the rooftop of her apartment building. As the perfumed tresses burst into flame, a great pillar of violet smoke rose into the sky and rained golden ash onto the Street below, where working girls and revellers looked up in awe, the glittering flakes falling on their palms.

Then the woman once known as Duchess Gloriana Cochrain aka Darren the hairdresser went back down to her apartment and shaved her skull bare. As she gazed at her face in the mirror, she vowed to herself that no one would ever hurt her again—and that she would not rest until every last drop of blood that had ever been spilled on the Street of Miracles was given the justice it was due.

from my notebook —

song of the pocket knife, part 4

little silver fang-friend,
could it be
that i
don't need you
anymore?

Overheard:
Lucretia and Valaria

The gang is training on the roof of the abandoned warehouse. Rapunzelle leads the girls through a series of kick-boxing drills. Valaria and Lucretia slip away from the group, murmuring conspiratorially. Lucretia catches me watching and shoots me Death Eyes. I look away, wait a few moments, and then sneak after them, using the Shadow Jutsu technique my father taught me to stay out of sight. Inside the hollowed-out factory shell, Valaria and Lucretia are arguing passionately.

VALARIA

Listen, you know what you signed up for. If you've lost the stomach for it, no one's holding a gun to your head. You can leave at any time. Run back to Kimaya and her little community centre like a scared bunny rabbit.

LUCRETIA
(in a screaming whisper)

I signed on to rough up a few dudebros and scare people enough to think twice about beating on femmes, not get into a vigilante gang war that's all over the news. This is getting out of hand, Val, and you know it.

VALARIA

This is going exactly where it needs to.

LUCRETIA

People are calling for doubled—tripled—police patrols on the Street! Regulars are staying away from the usual joints, and that means bad business for working girls and everyone else. We're hurting femmes more than we're helping them, and the Street will turn on us eventually. Probably sooner rather than later.

VALARIA

(a slight smile playing at the corners of her mouth)

What did you think? That we would mug a guy here and there, collect a couple wallets, spray-paint an alley wall and call it a day? You think too small, Luce, you always have. That's your problem. You're too invested in the way things are—your rich dates and the designer shoes they buy you. Never stopping to think that they should be the ones begging for your attention, indulging your kinks, living at your beck and call, not the other way around. You could set the master's house on fire, and instead you dance for scraps at his table.

LUCRETIA

I don't remember you giving me an empowerment feminism lecture when it was *your* kinks I was indulging!

VALARIA

So is that what this is about?

LUCRETIA

Don't you fucking dare say it.

VALARIA

You're jealous, aren't you?

LUCRETIA
(throwing up her arms)

What? Of who? Certainly not that little psycho killer baby you can't take your eyes off of. For one thing, she's jailbait. For another, she's a rabid bitch who loves violence. Come to think of it, you two deserve each other.

VALARIA
(smirking)

Well, you of all people know that I do appreciate a rabid bitch, Lulu.

LUCRETIA

Fuck you, Valaria. You walk around here thinking you're better than the rest of us with your big ideas and your stupid shaved head and your leather boots. Thinking you're some kind of revolutionary heroine and the rest of us your little soldiers. News flash: Some of us live in the real world. Some of us have real dreams. Some of us need more than fancy words and political masturbation to live on.

She starts to stomp away. Valaria lunges forward, grabs her arm, and spins her around roughly. Lucretia lashes back and slaps her across the face. They freeze in mid-struggle, panting.

VALARIA

There was a time when I thought I wanted to live in the real world, Lulu. But we live on the *Street* of *Miracles*. And ain't nobody here getting their dreams come true if we don't tear down this whole rotten world and make ourselves a new one. Tell me that isn't true, Lulu. I dare you.

LUCRETIA

Val...

VALARIA

I know that the reason things didn't work out between us is because you didn't believe that a new world is possible, Lulu.

LUCRETIA
(softly)

The reason things didn't work out between us is because you loved your imaginary revolution more than you loved me, Valkyrie.

(touching Valaria's cheek)

VALARIA

Valkyrie ... it's been a long time since you've called me that.

LUCRETIA
You've never stopped calling me Lulu.

They kiss. I'm full of a roiling energy that I don't know the name of. Fuck Lucretia. If she's not jealous of me, then I'm not jealous of her. Right? Or something. I slide away from the scene, back to the group.

Social Justice Warriors of the Ivory Tower

Soon the Lipstick Lacerators have become so infamous that we catch the attention of a group of revolutionary students and professors at the University. They call themselves the Social Justice Warriors of the Ivory Tower, and they want to write a book about us or something.

They get in touch with us through Ivana, who knows them because they once paid her a hundred bucks just to sit and talk about her life on tape, as research for a project they were doing on trans girls.

"I mostly just made everything up," she says, "but it was kind of fun, actually. They're okay types, and they have lots of money."

"It would be nice to get some good press, for once," says Rapunzelle.

Valaria nods. "This is a chance to get our message out from a different angle," she says, like the war strategist she is, "and to reach beyond the City of Smoke and Lights. Although I don't trust anyone with a PhD, so we'll have to be careful about what we say."

So we go to the University, which is way out on the

edge of the City of Smoke and Lights, far from the eternal nighttime and floating lanterns of the Street of Miracles. The campus buildings are huge and ancient and made of grey stone, grown over by long braids of tangled ivy. Bright sunlight turns the huge, manicured lawns a brilliant green. Carefully placed trees, shrubs, and fountains break up the landscape.

"It's so *fancy*," says Rapunzelle, looking around like someone who knows she isn't supposed to be here. The rest of us are doing the same thing, except for Lucretia, who goes to fancy places all the time, and Valaria, who always acts like she owns whatever place she's in.

The fingernails of a ghostly hand rake gently over the skin of my back. I was supposed to go to university. It was everything that my parents wanted, the reason they kept me locked up in their crooked house with nothing but books for friends.

I was supposed to be in a university like this, surrounded by grey stone and trees and libraries. Dressed like one of the hundreds of hipsters strolling around campus, with pointy leather shoes and hardcover textbooks.

And I don't want to want it, but I do: to be a part of this place.

The Social Justice Warriors of the Ivory Tower meet us in a private library tucked into the corner of a courtyard full of white flowers. The windows are stained glass, and colourful veils of light spill onto a massive oak table where we all sit.

There are eight of them: three professors and five students. They don't look like what I expect, which is more of the prepsters we saw outside. Instead they are wearing

T-shirts, old jeans, sneakers. One of the professors, a woman with short grey hair who looks about fifty, thanks us for coming and introduces everyone by their names (which I immediately forget) and "preferred pronouns."

I'm not sure what a preferred pronoun is, but I'm too embarrassed to ask. One of the students, a cute boy with brown hair, round cheeks, and the most adorable grin I've ever seen, notices my confusion. He winks at me and says, "Oh, just for those who aren't familiar, by preferred pronoun, we just mean whether someone prefers to be called he, she, they, or something else when being talked about in the third person."

Ivana snorts, as though she can't believe that university people have the time to worry about things like that. Valaria nods gravely, and says, "Thanks for the explanation. Let's talk about this book you are writing. Here's what we think it should say..."

The conversation is long and kind of boring, to tell the truth. Valaria and Rapunzelle do most of the talking for us femmes, since the other girls don't really care about books or writing that much. I do care—a lot, actually—about books, but I don't feel like I know enough yet to be a part of the conversation.

So instead, I sneak out of my chair and take a look at the library. There are so many books here—hundreds and hundreds—and this is just one library in a university full of them. Just looking at them, row after row of stuffed shelves gleaming in the rays of stained glass–coloured sunlight, makes my eyes water and my stomach hurt, and I am filled with a sharp, hungry wanting.

The boy with the round face finds me up on a second

floor, running my hand over the spines of a row of books, deciphering their titles.

"A girl who likes to read, huh?" he says. His eyes are big and light, light blue. They remind me of my little sister's eyes—her sweetness.

"You're surprised that girls read?" I retort. "Because *that's* a good pick-up line."

"No way," he says. "I used to be a girl who liked to read."

"Oh," I say, "I couldn't tell." And even though I know it's rude, I can feel my eyes sliding over his body, the same way that people's eyes sometimes slide over mine. Looking for signs of the past.

"Like what you see?" he asks, raising an eyebrow.

"I'm sorry," I say, blushing.

"Don't be," he says. "It's always nice to meet a fellow reader. Most university kids don't actually like to read at all."

"Really?" I say. And then again. "*Really?*"

"Yeah," he says, "they don't get books. They're just here because someone told them to be."

Like my parents told me to be. But like I want to be. Or maybe I don't. I don't belong in a university, but a part of me does. I don't know. My head hurts. A ghost hand tugs at my ankle. I ignore it.

"But you get books," I say, like a challenge.

"Yes," he says. "Books are like this magical window that you can open no matter where you are and you fall into a different place that's better than the one you're trapped in."

"Exactly," I say.

And I notice that somehow, the distance between us

has grown smaller. We are leaning very, very close together. His eyelashes are long and lovely.

The ghost hands yank sharply at the ends of my hair. Black bees buzz and crawl under my skin. I don't belong in this place, with this boy who used to be a girl who likes to read. Maybe there was a time when I would have, but not anymore.

"We should get back to the group," I say.

This is how the end begins:

It starts with a regular job, going after a skinny guy in a dress shirt and suit pants walking alone in an alley behind one of the bars where a lot of femmes go to work. An easy mark—too easy. Tonight, Ivana starts the hunt. As the rest of us wait in the shadows, she stalks the guy to the end of the alley, then rushes in holding a long wooden stick to trip him with.

A ghost hand yanks sharply on my earlobe, and I know, in the second before Ivana reaches the mark, that something is wrong. As I open my mouth to scream a warning, the mark spins around, a folding baton expanding in his fist, and knocks Ivana to the ground.

"PIGS!" screams Rapunzelle, but it's much too late. Most of us have already started emerging from the shadows to follow up Ivana's attack, and suddenly dozens of bulky figures in black armour are pouring out of the back doors that line the alley. Cop car lights flash at either end. They are all waving batons, and many are holding guns.

"FREEZE," a disembodied megaphone voice booms through the air.

"RUN!" yells Valaria, and in a move so fast I can barely

understand what is happening, she vaults forward to slam the cop who was our mark off his feet, throws Ivana over her shoulder, and drags her into the space between two buildings.

"FREEZE," the megaphone voice booms again, and then the air is exploding with the BANG BANG of gunshots and the air cracks and shatters like ice and the world spins wildly, out of control, and the girls are screaming running screaming running screaming screaming screaming rolling jumping climbing clawing fleeing into the crimson night as blinding police flashlight beams cut through the dark.

I am over the alley wall and hit the ground running running. My ankle twists and sends pain rattling through my leg body brain and I keep on going, zigzagging crazily, like a moth in the wind. Black clouds, thick and acrid, replace the normally perfumed scent of the Street, and my eyes pour tears.

Oh, please, please, if there is any magic in this world please let it save me. I am too young and too hungry to die yet I know I know every femme knows what happens to tranny girls caught by the pigs.

I hit the busiest part of the Street of Miracles and sprint on, jackknifing and dodging through the crowd of pleasure seekers, ignoring their shouts of surprise and outrage. I can hear the heavy boots of the cops hitting the ground behind me.

"STOP OR WE'LL SHOOT," one of them says, but I keep going, throat burning. They won't shoot with all of the civilians around. Will they?

Above us, the cloud layer splits open, and a full moon

the colour of rust shines incandescent onto the Street of Miracles. In the weird light, the Street seems to twist and writhe, doubling back on itself in infinite loops, so that the normally straight road is full of hidden corners and un-expected turns. Despite the fact that I must be slowing down, the sound of the heavy boots on pavement recedes further and further behind me, and I realize that the Street is helping, helping me get away.

I stagger on, until I think that I have lost them. Still following the Street, which at this point has become an entirely unfamiliar shape, I stumble into a small, high-walled courtyard that I have never seen before. In the centre, there is an empty fountain with a huge shape in the middle, but it is so overrun with vines that I can't tell what it's supposed to be.

I fall to my knees, palms on the ground, gasping for breath. The fountain looms. Over and over, I suck air into my lungs. *It's over, it's over,* I tell myself.

And just as I have stood back up to figure out what to do next, I hear footsteps on the mazelike path behind me.

A high-pitched voice that can only belong to a femme cuts through the air. "Let go of me, you fucking pig!" yells Lucretia.

"SHUT UP FAGGOT," the cop yells back, and there is a bone-crunching sound, followed by Lucretia's scream as she is dragged into the courtyard by an arm that hangs at an impossible angle from her torso. The cop is hitting her across the face with a baton, pausing only to glance up at the fountain, the courtyard, the bizarre copper moon. I am hidden by the statue, and neither of them sees me there.

Lucretia starts laughing then, long and loud and high-pitched hysterical laughter. "The First Femme will curse you," she snarls, and spits into the cop's face. "Don't you know where you are?" And I can tell that the cop is unnerved—by the moon, by the fountain, by Lucretia's demonic bravado—because he falls silent for a second, glancing from side to side.

In that moment he looks young, somehow, instead of stony and ageless like most cops look to me. Young and, well, scared.

"What the fuck is this place?" he says, and I can hear the nervousness creeping into his voice. He must have gotten separated from his pack of goons while chasing Lucretia.

Lucretia keeps laughing, blood rattling in her throat. "This is the Street of Miracles, asshole," she rasps. "This place belongs to faggots and trannies, and after tonight, it's never going to let you go."

The cop roars and hurls Lucretia on the ground. Her usually perfect blond mane flies up in a cloud around her face. He throws his baton onto the ground and reaches into his belt. He is going for the gun, pulling it out, to shoot Lucretia shoot Lucretia shoot Lucretia, and why shouldn't he? No one will care about another dead tranny killed on the Street of Miracles.

And then my body is moving, moving, faster than I can understand or control and I feel myself dive forward. Roll over the ground and snatch up the baton. Come up silent and ferocious and hit the cop from behind, right across the back of the head, just as he is bringing out his gun.

It sounds like an eggshell breaking. Then he crumples to the ground, a puppet with the strings cut, his head bouncing off the edge of the fountain as he does. He lands with his neck folded unnaturally, blood pooling to form a dark puddle that oozes slowly across the ground, glinting in the rusty moonlight.

And at last, everything is quiet and still.

Blood spilled on the Street of Miracles

Oh my god, I just killed a cop. I just killed a cop."
Maybe it'll stop being real if I just keep on saying it,
over and over. But the body of the policeman just stays
sprawled there at the base of the fountain, his neck bent
in half like a snapped tree branch. I give him a kick in the
crotch to see if that will produce anything, but he is well
and truly dead.

"What the fuck am I gonna do?"

Only the wind answers. I drop to the ground, shivering, breathing hard. What to do. What to do. I glance over
at Lucretia. She's lying on her stomach, and she's so still
that for a second I think that she's dead, too.

Then she stirs, just a little. I admit I'm relieved.

Lucretia tries to drag herself up from the ground
where the cop threw her. There's blood and dirt and
phlegm all over her, and her arm looks pretty fucked up,
so I go over to help. She flinches when I reach out, but she
isn't really getting anywhere by herself, so she eventually
lets me haul her onto her feet.

"Thanks," she mutters, not looking me in the eye.

"What am I gonna do," I say again. There's blood on

my hands and arms and clothes and it's cold and I'm shaking so hard I can hardly stand, and I can barely breathe because of the pounding in my chest and for the first time, I wish that I had never come here to this city full of smoke and light and lost souls.

"Oh god, oh god, oh god, oh god," I say, sinking onto my knees in front of the fountain.

"Will you just stop for a second," says Lucretia. There's a shadow of the old, snotty tone in her voice again. "You're not helping anything."

I respond with fists clenched. "If you hadn't been such a dumb-ass bitch and gotten caught, then I never would've hit him in the first place."

"I didn't ask you to murder anyone, you psycho," she snaps back, and then I really lose it.

"HE WAS GONNA SHOOT YOU, YOU VAPID FUCKING WASTE OF OXYGEN," I say. "Maybe I should have let him. You think you're so great with your stupid makeup and your stupid hair and your stupid boobs and your stupid clothes that your stupid fucking boyfriends pay for. Well, fuck you, Lucretia. You may think you're the centre of the goddamn fucking universe and everyone's jealous of you, but you know what? Everyone on the whole goddamn Street of Miracles thinks you're a fucking cunt. And now they're gonna find his body and I'm gonna go to jail and get fucking raped and die there all because I saved your stupid worthless bitchy ass," I finish, breathing heavily.

For a second, Lucretia just stares at me in total silence. Her beat-up doll face is totally expressionless, except for a slight twitching in her cheek. The moonlight glints off her blue eyes.

Then she says, quietly, "You're not going to jail. You're going to be fine."

"What?" I say.

"I know you think I'm a bitch," she says, and she sounds almost sad. "I know the other girls think that, too. I'm not stupid, you know. I saw how happy they were when you beat me up that time at FAB."

A hot and ugly feeling worms its way through my anger and fear, a giant caterpillar wriggling around in my stomach. The caterpillar is saying, *She's right. You liked beating her up. You like hurting people. That's why you killed that cop; it wasn't to save Lucretia, that's for sure. You're not the kind of girl who saves people.*

You're the kind who kills them.

"I only did that because you made fun of my boobs," I say, but it comes out limply, and Lucretia ignores me.

"Well, maybe I am a bitch," she says. "You can say whatever you want about me, but at least I'm honest about who I am. I don't pretend to be something that I'm not, like Kimaya always trying to save everyone or Valaria acting like she's a big-shot revolutionary, or you pretending like you're some big tough girl when you clearly haven't got a clue what you're doing. I tell it like it is, and I get what I want, and no one on this whole damn planet can tell me that's wrong. Not after what I've lived through."

She pauses for breath.

Then she says, "And you're not going to jail because I'm going to turn myself in and tell them that I did it. I'll take his badge with me, to prove it. I'll say that he caught me and broke my arm and he was gonna shoot me, and I got his baton away from him and hit him in self-defence."

"That isn't ... that's not going to work," I say, through the roaring in my ears. Whenever blood is shed on the Street of Miracles, it's trans girls who pay, in the end. I just never thought it would be *Lucretia*.

"I can't let you do this," I say.

"Fuck that," Lucretia says, stamping her foot and cursing in pain as the motion jars her mangled arm. "You think that this is about you? You don't get it. You don't get to be my *rescuer*," she spits. "It's my mess—I'll clean it up. Besides," she says, one corner of her lips lifting slightly, "I'm a pretty white girl, right? Maybe they'll go easy on me."

I start to laugh, but it turns into a sob. I want to reach out and hug her. I want to turn and run away. In the distance, I can hear the sound of sirens—

No, wait. That's not what happened.

This is what happened:

"I'm gonna go to jail and get fucking raped and die there all because I saved your stupid worthless bitchy ass," I finish, breathing heavily.

For a second, Lucretia just stares at me in total silence. Her beat-up doll face is totally expressionless, except for a slight twitching in her cheek. The moonlight glints off her blue eyes.

Then, suddenly, those eyes widen. Her perfect bee-stung lips part in a gasp. "Look," Lucretia says, pointing behind me with her good arm.

I turn. All around me, the darkness rustles. For a moment, I do not understand. And then I see: the vines all over the courtyard, that cover the walls and the fountain, are moving.

"Fuck," I scramble backward, but the vines don't even come near me. Instead, they slither to wrap themselves around the body of the dead policeman, twining themselves through his limbs and over his torso and face until he is totally covered in them. The vines start to retract, and both Lucretia and I step back hastily, as the corpse of the policeman is drawn over the ground and up into the fountain.

At the same time, the vines cocooning the shape at the centre of the fountain unravel and fall away, revealing what they've been hiding:

Standing there on a plinth, shining beneath the stars, is a stone statue of an enormous woman with a round belly and giant breasts. Her eyes are closed, a beatific expression on her face. She is wearing a sleeveless dress with a flowing train and plunging neckline that shows off her Adam's apple like a magnificent jewel, and her hair falls in ringlets to her waist. She is so beautiful that I can only stare, stunned.

"It's *her*," Lucretia says, and I don't need to ask who. There is only one person, one Femme, this could be. As we watch, transfixed, the vines continue to recoil, drawing the policeman's body deeper and deeper into the well of the fountain—so deep that we can no longer see it.

The statue's eyes open. Lucretia and I scream and grab each other, but the First Femme doesn't move. Her expression remains serene and understanding. Water begins to run down her stone cheeks, in a trickle at first, then in rivulets, then steady streams. It gushes over the curves and valleys of her body, and into the well, which fills up impossibly quickly.

The fountain bubbles and gurgles as the water continues to flow, and the vines draw deeper and deeper into the earth. Suddenly, I am not afraid anymore, though a strange numbness remains where the feeling was. Lucretia and I step forward and touch the water, which is warm.

Without speaking, we wash the blood from each other's skin and hair. Even the stains on our clothes fade away as if they've never been.

Time dilates and eddies around us. The moon remains stationary in the sky. We are there for an eternity, for only a moment. We are safe. The only sounds are our breathing, our heartbeats, the song of the fountain.

When we are ready, we step back and look up at the face of the statue.

"Thank you," Lucretia whispers. And maybe it's a trick of the light, but for a second, the First Femme seems to be smiling back.

Side by side, Lucretia and I walk out of the courtyard to face the City once more.

Our bodies are bombs

I have to leave town for a while," Valaria tells me. We are standing beneath a bridge near the Harbour at the mouth of the river. Dozens of ships used to dock here every day to take shelter from winter storms, but now the Harbour stands deserted and the wood of the docks is rotting. Beneath the night sky, the water looks like melted glass.

It's been two weeks since the police set a sting for us, and since I've last seen Valaria. I've spent that time hiding in Kimaya's apartment, scared to go home, sleeping on the sofa and wracked by nightmares. I can't stop dreaming about zombie policemen, rotting corpses clawing up from wells in the centre of the earth to drag me away.

Sometimes, I dream about the cop I killed. About his family, waiting and waiting for him to come home. Since his body still hasn't been found, and I'm starting to believe it never will, he hasn't been declared murdered. There were a couple of stories in the paper (I scour the news every day) about a cop going missing during a "routine mission," but the story is so bizarre that there hasn't been a big reaction to it.

His name was Tyler. Tyler Rosen. No one but Lucretia and I knows what happened to him that night.

Incredibly, none of the Lipstick Lacerators were caught during the sting on the Street of Miracles. Somehow, despite some extremely close calls and quite a few injuries, every single one of us got away. According to Kimaya, some people are whispering that it is the magic of the Street, protecting us.

Others say it's because all through the pleasure district, trans femmes are standing together and refusing to give up our names. Everyone has been hit hard since the sting: love hotels, massage parlours, strip joints, all raided by the cops in the last two weeks. Countless femmes have been picked up off the Street and questioned, but no matter how badly the cops shake them down, no one seems to know the identities of the notorious Lipstick Lacerators.

Which isn't to say that we've gotten away with anything, necessarily. After getting hit in the head with a baton, Ivana gets dizzy spells and can't remember basic things, like other people's names or what day it is. Ying broke her ankle jumping over a fence, and now she's struggling to walk. Kiki can't see out of her left eye, having been sprayed right in the face.

Worst of all, Kimaya and Rapunzelle aren't speaking to each other. Kimaya says that she can't forgive Rapunzelle for risking her life like that and putting all of us in danger. She says it makes it even more terrible that Rapunzelle dragged me along into it. I try to tell Kimaya that it wasn't like that, but she just turns away and pretends like I haven't said anything.

And now, it's become almost impossible for femmes to work on the Street of Miracles. Everywhere we go, there are cops. Managers are scared to hire us, for anything.

Even the shadiest hotels won't rent us rooms. We stay shut up in our homes, waiting for something to happen. For our luck to change.

"I'm getting out of the City," Valaria tells me. "The word is that the cops have my description and are offering bribes to people on the Street to rat me out. Someone already told them I was the ringleader. I don't know how much longer I can stay under the radar. Things are getting too intense."

I look at Valaria, her tall, muscular frame and her shaved head. She's so recognizable, it's kind of amazing that she hasn't been caught already.

"Where are you going?" I ask, mostly because I don't know what else to say.

"Anywhere. Wherever. Who cares?" she says. "That's not what I wanted to talk to you about."

Earlier today, a big black bird came swooping down to land outside the window of Kimaya's apartment. It tapped on the glass with its beak until I went to open it. Tied around its leg with a piece of string was a rolled-up note that said, "Meet me at the Harbour at midnite. - V."

"Don't go," Kimaya had said. "Hasn't she gotten you in enough trouble already?"

But I had to. I was in this deep already, wasn't I? There was no turning back from what I'd done, not anymore. I killed that cop. Watched his body get wrapped in vines and vanish into the belly of that fountain.

"So, what did you want to talk about?" I ask Valaria, shivering slightly in the wind, which is blowing cold off the surface of the river.

"I can't lead the girls anymore," she says. "At least, not

right now. I'll be back, but I don't know when yet, and that means someone has to take over. Someone has to keep fighting." She looks at me pointedly.

"What? Me? Why?" I ask. I've never wanted to lead anything in my life.

Valaria smiles slightly. "You're smart. You're brave. You're the best fighter out of all of us, even me. And you've got that fire," she says, "burning inside you. You want justice, and you're willing to do what it takes to get it."

"No," I say, shaking my head. "No, you—you're wrong. I'm not that person. And I don't want to fight anymore, not like this. Never again. I can't. I can't. I can't! I didn't think it was going to be like this. I just—I just wanted to be a part of something. To feel strong. But I don't feel strong, I feel sick."

And what I don't say is, *I feel tired. I don't want to be myself anymore.*

Valaria watches me calmly. Her voice is gentle as she says, "You're stronger than you think." She puts a hand on my shoulder. "And you and I both know that you were born to fight, to show this awful world what it means to be a trans girl who hits back. This is war, and you were made to be a soldier in it. You can't change that, not even if you wanted to."

"No," I say, "you're wrong about me. I'm never going to hurt anyone—ever again."

"Yes, you will," Valaria says simply. "There's no turning back now. Not after what you did to that cop. You think I don't know that was you? You aren't a little girl anymore. You've gotten your hands dirty, and you have a responsibility to your sisters to finish what we started."

"You don't know me," I say, but the words are very thin. I fix my eyes on hers.

"I know you," Valaria says, and she reaches out, pulls me close. "I know you," she whispers again, lips brushing against my cheek.

And then she kisses me, a kiss that is deep and ferocious. A kiss about the shock of the impact of bodies, slamming together. A kiss about warrior femmes, bodies painted bright for combat, about writhing snakelike on the dance floor of the battleground. About catching the fist before it hits your face and twisting back the arm that tried to hurt you till it breaks. About refusing ever, ever to forget all the femmes that fought and died before us, about screaming their names to the distant stars.

The kiss goes on and on, deeper and deeper. Clouds of thick black bees swarm up in my lower body, roil in my stomach, crawl up my throat, buzzing angrily. My bones vibrate and rattle. I cannot think, cannot speak. Valaria has one hand on the back of my head, the other on my lower spine. She pulls me closer to her, and my body is screaming screaming. My body is a bomb, it's going to explode with rage and pleasure and wanting and memory and fear.

No, I whisper, but it's only in my head, and Valaria keeps on going, dragging her hot wet lips down my chin and over my throat.

No, I try again, but my traitor mouth doesn't have the word, has never known the word, has only known how to lie, and *no* is a true word and it doesn't belong to me.

No no no no no no no NO the word rips like a hurricane through the tender flesh underneath my skin, but I cannot say it do not say it have never been able to say anything when it really counts. Words have always failed me, I have always failed words, my body is bad it is dangerous it is a bomb about to explode and now her fingers are trickling trickling trickling down my abdomen into my pants—

"NO," I scream, and before I know what I'm doing, my hands are talking for me talking for me making fists and slashing up through the air to strike Valaria in the face right, left, right, just like my father taught me once.

Blood and a tooth spray through the air. Valaria's head snaps back, and she reels, stumbling away from me. Her arms pinwheel, she sways, and for one terrible moment I think that I have killed her too, but she recovers her balance and settles back on her feet, cradling her chin with her hands.

"I'm sorry," I say. Valaria laughs. Blood and phlegm gurgle in her throat and she spits it out onto the ground.

"See that?" she says. "You're a fighter all right. That's my girl."

And she turns away with a swagger, leaving me breathless and wordless and afraid of myself in the dark.

Dream diary, or, Sympathy for the zombie

The dream is always different, but the dream is always the same.

I am always waiting somewhere—in the woods with the coyotes, in the playground behind my parents' house, in the alley behind FAB, in the warehouse headquarters of the Lipstick Lacerators. I am waiting and I am alone. I cannot leave. Or maybe I can, but I choose not to. Or maybe it's the same thing. I'm not sure. Either way, I'm going nowhere.

And it wouldn't matter even if I was going somewhere, because in the dream, I am being followed by something that I can't outrun. That I can't escape. No matter where I go, no matter where I look, I can always see it, see him, in my peripheral vision.

Him. The cop. The monster. The zombie. Tyler. The cop I killed.

His body starts out rotting and horrible—full of pits and gaping holes, exposed organs the colour of raw, putrid meat. His bones make squelching and popping sounds as he propels them into motion through the stiffness of desiccated cartilage. His head is caved in from where I hit it with the baton and hangs at that unnatural angle. But that isn't even the most terrible thing.

As he gets closer and closer, he starts to heal. The ragged edges of the holes smooth and close, his flesh reknits itself and blooms into living colour. His neck rights itself and his skull mends, covered by glinting golden hair. His eyes shine bright blue.

I ought to scream. I ought to run. I ought to put up my fists, at least. But I don't. I don't. I don't.

By the time he reaches me, his body is fresh and perfectly formed in the image of blond, muscled, porn-star masculinity. Like a fascist angel. His tattered uniform falls away and crumbles to dust, and then his underwear. His dick juts out from his abdomen, like a stabbing weapon. He looms naked in front of me, huge and menacing.

I do not move do not breathe do not say do not speak. Bees buzz bees buzz bees buzz bees buzz all through my dream body up and down up and down.

"Hello again," he says. "Do you remember me?"

And I can only say, "I do."

And he says, "I can't believe you killed me."

And I say, "I had to. To save Lucretia."

"Please," he says. "You wanted to save Lucretia? Wasn't that you, twisting her arm and pinning her down, dominating her, hurting her, and loving it? Just like I did. Just like me."

"No," I say, but he ignores me.

"You killed me to become me," he goes on. "You killed me so that you could have my strength."

"You don't know anything about me," I say.

"Of course I do," he answers, and his voice is gentle, like a lover's. "I know you. Your whole life you've been this small, terrified thing, straining to remake yourself in the image of something that you know you'll never become. Longing for the power to make other people afraid, because that's the only way you know to get rid of the fear in yourself. You hit people because you hate your body. You hate people like Lucretia, people you think are beautiful, because you don't love yourself. I know all about wanting to be strong. Believe me."

"No," I whisper. Oh wait. No I don't. I don't say anything at all.

"You were the real monster all along," he says, and then he is kissing me, kissing me, with his hot invader's tongue, the muscled slopes of his naked rolling desert body pressing up against mine, and the killer swarm is raging inside me, I should break his grip, break his arms, crush his windpipe, but I don't I don't...

Because then I am him and he is me, and it's his razor-angled Asian body I am holding in my muscled, blond-haired arms; it's his longish black hair that I am caressing in my heavy-knuckled hands, his slender hips that I am grinding my larger ones against, and my killer cop cop killer body that is stirring blazing devouring devouring devouring devouring swallowing him/her/me whole.

And then I wake up SCREAMING SCREAMING SCREAMING SCREAMING, except no sound leaves my mouth, my body bucking and heaving with the force of those silent screams, shuddering with my gasping breaths, full of a buzzing swarm of killer bees.

from my notebook —

song of the pocket knife, part 5

so silly to think
that i could ever leave you
behind, little razor smile,
so stupid to believe
that i would grow up
and away
from needing you,
your kisses,
slicing up
and down
my arms,
my thighs,
the places
no one can see,
sorry that
i ever thought
of giving you up,
no one understands me like you do,
no one knows
how to keep me
in line
like you,

if i hadn't stopped believing
in you, pocket knife,
maybe i wouldn't be
in so much trouble now,
i know that you
can't make it better,
you can't fix
what's always been
broken,
but still,
i deserve this,
you.

Dear Charity,

I'm sorry that things have been so hard for you at home, what with you being suspended and getting into fights with Mom and all. And I guess I should have known better than to send you cigarettes and not expect you to smoke them. That was pretty dumb of me.

I know that you're not very happy with me right now, and that this probably isn't what you want to hear from me, but I guess I keep on thinking of you as my kid sister, you know? In some ways, I think I needed you to keep on being this sweet, tiny little girl I used to take care of and protect all the time, because being your big sister was the only thing that I felt like I was doing right in this world.

And I guess I still needed to feel that, even after I left.

But I think the thing is, Charity, that what we both really need is for me to stop taking care of you so much and start taking better care of me. Because we both have to learn how to take care of ourselves, if that makes any sense.

And if learning to take care of yourself means that you've got to smoke a few cigarettes and

punch a few snotty white girls in the face,
well, I probably shouldn't, like, endorse that or
anything, but I'm not going to rag on you about it
either.

I wish I could come and see you too, but things
are really busy over here right now, what with
work shifts and the exam for my French class
and all. It's all pretty boring. No sex or drugs or
rock n roll or vigilante gang violence or zombie
ghost men coming back from the dead to haunt
my waking nightmares ha ha ha ha ha.

If you need me, you know where I am: first star
to the right and straight on till the dark becomes
light.

Love,

Your sister

ps: I'm putting this rose quartz crystal and some
shiny fabric into the envelope for your collection.
My friend Kimaya made me a dress out of the
fabric.

PART IV: FORGIVENESS

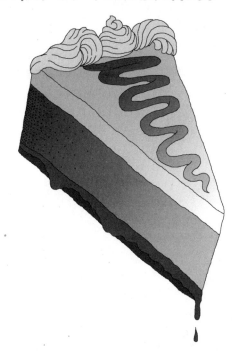

Alzena the Witch's house

Alzena the Witch's house is full of wonderful and mysterious objects: candles, crystals balls, packs of yellowing Tarot cards, antique clocks without hands, carved wooden boxes, jars full of dried leaves and flowers, dolls tied up and hung from the ceiling with pieces of string. These things cover every available surface in the tiny house wrapped in its tiny weed garden, and fill the cramped rooms with shadows and dust.

Alzena makes me sit at a wobbly table in her kitchen and wait for her to make tea before answering my question. We do not talk while she boils the water and scoops the tea into a little wooden basket that she lowers into a battered Chinese teapot that reminds me of my mother.

The tea is made from the petals of a spiky purple flower, and the scent is sugar violets with a hint of vinegar. The liquid that Alzena pours into my cup is a bright amethyst. When I taste it, I start to cry silently, but I don't know why. I haven't cried for as long as I can remember.

"That's normal," Alzena says, to explain. "This is a crying tea." She sips hers, and a single, elegant tear rolls out of one of her tilted golden eyes.

"It's good for you," she says, "to cry sometimes. Even

if there isn't a reason."

Alzena the Witch is strange and keeps mostly to herself. Unlike most of the trans girls I know, she doesn't work as a hostess or waitress or dancer, or take clients in sleazy hotels. They say that Alzena doesn't work at all. Instead, she stays here in this house, collecting things and casting spells, which she says she sees as her sacred calling rather than mundane labour.

Alzena has a talent for knowing and doing things that no one else can. She can tell you what the weather will be like two weeks from now, or if you're about to make a bunch of cash on a date. She knows exactly where your good-for-nothing roommate's run off to with a stash of your drugs.

Alzena can make it rain just by combing her long, thick hair. If you piss her off, the girls say, she can cast a curse on you to make you trip and break your ankle or grow a thick, untameable beard overnight.

But the most powerful magic Alzena has is to make someone fall in love. She can do it just by pointing one of her long, slender fingers or with a glance of her golden eyes. This is the magic that has made Alzena famous among the femmes of the City—because she'll do it for you, if you ask. She'll make someone fall in love with you, anyone you want.

They say that when Alzena the Witch was younger, she was the most beautiful femme on the Street of Miracles, with her lustrous copper skin and generous breasts. They say that one night, she closed her luminous eyes and wished for a handsome, rich man to take her away from the poverty and desperation that she lived in.

Someone who would give her a house and all the money she could ever need. And he came—the only catch was, he was already married to a nice white lady in the suburbs.

Alzena is still beautiful, but her face is covered with lines. There are yellow bruises on her copper skin, a tracery of fingerprints on her throat and wrists.

Once Alzena makes someone fall in love with you, no one can make them stop.

Alzena takes a lock of my hair in return for answering my question. This worries me a little, but she reassures me that she will only use it for good spells.

"I gave up curses a long time ago," she says.

I am expecting her to gaze into one of her crystal balls, or consult her Tarot cards, or at least read my palm. But she doesn't do any of those things. Instead, she just looks at me as though she is staring through my skull and into my brain. It is a look that makes me shiver and squirm, while the amethyst tea continues to make tears slide down my face.

In that moment, I believe that Alzena the Witch can see everything about me. She knows that I can't sleep anymore, that every time I try I get terrible nightmares about zombie policemen. She knows that I can't eat or drink, and that sometimes I shake uncontrollably and fall to the ground like maybe I am possessed.

She knows that I am filled with secrets and bloodlust and killer bees, and that everything I touch falls apart.

But even though she can see all of these things, Alzena doesn't look disgusted or pitying. She just looks. After a while, she puts a hand on my cheek. Her fingers are cool and dry.

"You will be able to stop hurting people when you can stop hurting yourself," she says.

I sit there, turning the words over in my mind. "But how do I do that?" I say, finally.

Alzena shakes her head. Thick black curls tumble past her shoulders in a glossy waterfall. She looks up at her menagerie of strange, lonely objects: the clocks, the jars, the boxes, the dolls, the candles and crystals and cards. Then she looks down at the bruises on her wrists.

"If I knew that magic," she says, "I wouldn't be here anymore."

Open mic night at the Cabaret Rouge

W hat we need," Kimaya says, "is a storytelling night."

I look over at Kimaya from her sofa, where I've been crashing since everything went down, and from which I've barely moved in that time.

"A storytelling night?" I repeat, not understanding. It's been three months since the cop ambush and the Lipstick Lacerators disbanded, followed by Valaria the Goddess of War leaving town to go who knows where. Three months since the police started making the Street of Miracles almost impossible to live in. Except we have nowhere else to go.

"A good story can fix anything," Kimaya nods firmly, the beads in her braids clattering.

Even your relationship with Rapunzelle? is what I think but do not say. Kimaya is still refusing to talk to her former girlfriend, even though Rapunzelle keeps on leaving notes and flowers and homemade baked goods on her doorstep. Kimaya won't even look at them.

"Throw them in the trash," she tells me, chin raised. But Rapunzelle won't take no for an answer.

"I'm dying without her," she told me once through the window, pressing her nose up against the screen. "You've got to convince her to just talk to me, please."

But Kimaya is implacable. "She made her choice," she keeps on saying, "and it wasn't me. I'm too old for girls who want to throw their lives away."

It's true that no one is more committed to life than Kimaya. The moment she gets up, she rinses her face in rose and lavender water. She puts flowers in her hair and dresses in bright colors, no matter what. Even with police raids choking all of the business on the Street, she finds a way to book the Cabaret Rouge for a private night, for free.

"The manager owes me a favour," she says, refusing to tell me why. She spends the whole day calling the girls, telling each one that she's hosting an open mic night— private, just for trans girls. She asks them about their lives, how they're doing in these hard times. She tells them how much she's missed them, how good it would be to see them soon.

How can someone so kind and tender be so cruel to Rapunzelle?

On the night of the open mic, Kimaya drags me off the sofa, runs a comb through my hair and dresses me up in the dark crimson dress. "You are coming with me," she says, "no ifs ands or buts, missy."

"But I don't wanna go out," I whine, and she pinches my arm with her long, glittery gel nails. All tenderness has limits.

The Cabaret Rouge is the oldest theatre in the plea- sure district and is steeped in legend and mystery. Rumour has it that eighty years ago, the wealthiest businessman in the City had it built just so that he could dress up in gowns made of satin and ostrich feathers and dance wearing a headdress made of tropical fruit.

We enter through the back entrance because we don't want anyone to know that an event is happening here. The floorboards creak under our footsteps, and above us, the crystals on ancient chandeliers chime. The stage is mounted in a classic proscenium arch covered with gold-painted mouldings, and the backdrop is a lurid red velvet. To my surprise, the place is packed with trans girls, some of whom I haven't seen in weeks, and some I've never seen before at all.

Dust rises like ghosts.

I look around and I see Noor, Morena, Laurentine to my left. Ivana, Ying, and Alzena to my right. Gwen. Luxe, the new girl with frightened eyes, who just arrived from a city far away. Ancient Marie-Eve, reclining in her seat like a queen on her throne. Dozens of others, whom I can't believe I don't know yet. Far in the back, Rapunzelle sits in a corner, trying to shrink down her massive body.

A spotlight hits the stage and Kimaya emerges, swathed in glittering gold fabric. Her braids are caught up in a shimmering net of paste jewels. She has never looked more beautiful.

"Dear femmes," she says, "I've brought us all together on this darkest of nights so we can tell our stories. We live in difficult and dangerous times, it is true. But as long we have our stories, and we have each other, then we have hope. And this is the greatest magic of all."

And then music begins to play, and Kimaya dances. I've never seen her dance before. She moves like something ferocious, something powerful, like something sinuous and earthy and full of fire. In her movements, there is everything that my body feels and has never been able to say. She sweeps her hand and the sky falls like a curtain. She stomps her foot and the earth shakes.

When Kimaya is done, the other femmes go up, one by one. Most dance, sing, or lip-sync. Some read poems or tell stories. As the night goes on, something grows between us, something strange and penetrating and powerful. I glance around the room. Everywhere I look, the women are crying, silently, like the First Femme in her secret fountain. I touch my cheeks. They're wet.

"Who knew that we had all this talent," murmurs Ivana, who is sitting to my right.

"It's ... incredible," whispers Ying, sniffling in her seat next to Ivana.

"But femmes perform all the time on the Street," I protest.

To my left, Noor shakes her magnificent head. "Not like this," she says. "Not just for ourselves, for each other, instead of for some guy who wants to buy us or make money off of us."

Each performance reaches deep inside me and opens me up. Words flow silently like clear salt water through my pores.

And then Kimaya is smiling and holding the microphone out to me and waving me over. I guess it's my turn. I don't want to get up, but then my feet are moving for me. Ghost hands tug on my wrist, pulling me on. Bees buzz and rattle in my guts. I ascend the stage, palms sweaty and throat dry.

Kimaya hands me the mic. Before stepping down into the audience, she squeezes my arm. A pulse of heat radiates up from her fingers and through my shoulder into my body. It cracks the ice cubes in my blood.

I turn to face the audience. I look my sisters in the eye: They are warm. Rowdy. Tender. Tough. Generous. Jealous. Everything.

I open my mouth and begin to speak.

from my notebook —

long hair

slowly,
slowly,
little by
little,
my hair

takes hold, grows longer,

grows curious, grows bold.

quietly,

meekly,

almost unnoticeably, my hair

creeps its way

past my earlobes, my throat, my shoulders, and
collarbone.

my hair is dreaming itself

longer and freer, wilder and tangled,

it dreams itself snarled and knotted and
restlessly windblown.

my hair is dreaming and becoming, becoming
and dreaming, dreaming and becoming and
becoming and becoming.

my hair is becoming long enough

to fall stubbornly into my face whenever i am
eating,

to get caught in my food and caught between
my lips, twisted round my fork like strands of
spaghetti,

my hair is becoming long enough

to fall past my chin, pull back in a ponytail,
to twirl round my fingers as i am thinking of
everyone i have ever left behind,

my hair is becoming heavy,

like the air in my father's kitchen after my
mother has slapped him across the face, a
thickness like thunder

waiting to BOOM its way out of the clouds,

my hair is becoming thick,

like the trees in the park behind my parents'
house where i escape to at night to climb up
into the gnarled hands of the branches to cling
beneath the moon and count my breathing while
listening to the sound of the coyote's howls,

yes, my hair is growing longer,

long enough to hide my eyes behind like a
curtain of clouds pulled shut over the moon.
long enough to drape around me in a silken
blanket to keep out the winter's teeth, to wrap
around my loved ones and keep them safe,

long enough

to tie up in a sinuous braid and wind around
my head like a circlet of rose vines, to twine into
a love-me-knot, a witch-knot, into nine magic
knots, to bring what i want to me and bind it
close to my heart forever and ever and ever,

as long

as a tall tale, a fishy story, fat and flapping its
fins, as long and sinuous as a serpent forking
its tongue. as long as the threads of a web of
lies, silken, barely visible, shimmering like
temptation in the orchard of desire, sticky as

hope and inevitable as despair, a web to fall into
like falling in love, to get caught and trapped in
all the while knowing that it was made of your
own spinning,
my hair

is going to be long enough

to let down and unwind like your spine
unwinding after a twelve-hour shift and no
cigarette breaks. to unravel like a good old yarn
finally coming right, to sweep out in a long
flowing mass and drag a comb through over and
over, like a sea hag summoning the storm,

my hair

is going to be so long

that it will fall like a river, flowing endlessly and
relentlessly, will race over land and cut through
mountains, unstoppable in its glory, in its search
for its mother, its search for the healing sea,

my hair will be dark enough

to pool like shadows pooling round the kitchen
table as the summer evening grows long and you
wait, hour after hour, for your lover to return.
dark as the memories swimming up like bitter
taffy in the back of your throat, dark as the places

you go in that moment between wakefulness and falling asleep, as the nothingness you sometimes imagine might be a better place to be in than here, dark like the nighttime and the loneliness settling into your bones,
and it will be soft

like her lips running over the tiny hairs on the back of your neck. soft as her palms, slick with wanting, sliding over your thighs and into your body, soft as the sounds she makes as she pushes inside you, soft as believing that some things can last,

long enough

to drape through the window and slither over land and float through the sea and tangle up ships and bring them to land,

to reach into the depths and bring up treasures long forgotten—an ancient statue, a sunken cathedral, a trunk full of pearls and Spanish doubloons,

to curl around the world like the snake that some people say gave birth to all life,

to unfurl like a giant fishing net across the sky and catch all the stars as they race through the heavens,

to spill like the galaxy unfolding, like the Milky
Way spreading, so the ancient Chinese lovers of
legend could walk across the bridge of heavens
to find each other once again,

to slide under doors and into corners, through
cracks in the sidewalk and holes in the ground.
to slip into the silent place, the hiding place,
the place where lost sisters go and wrap threads
round their wrists and guide them back to the
place where things live,

to reach back through time, and through
memory, and time, to race back through time and
find the ancestors singing, to bind us once more
to words flowing in their arteries and veins, to
bring back their blood into our hollow haunted
hearts and make us all whole at last.

yes, my hair,

my hair,

someday

soon

my hair

will be long enough.

Overheard: Kimaya and Rapunzelle

I'm lying on Kimaya's sofa bed, having just awoken from a fresh nightmare of Tyler Rosen lurching up out of a bottomless pit full of snaking vines when, over the pounding of my rabbity heart, I hear voices: through the flower-shaped protective bars on the window, which Kimaya has propped open with a stick, two femmes are whispering in hushed stage whispers (there isn't a femme in the world who would know how to really whisper if her life depended on it). From the sounds of it, the drama is playing out from right below the window:

"I told you not to show your sorry-ass face around here anymore," one of them says in a low, throaty rumble laced with an unmistakable island accent.

"Baby, come on, I've said I'm sorry a thousand times," Rapunzelle's voice is a higher-pitched whine, a voice that has lost much of its strength, if not its edge.

KIMAYA

And you can say it a thousand more and shove it up your

ass. We're through, Rapunzelle.

RAPUNZELLE

Because I decided to fight back? You're punishing me because I stood up for myself? For Ivana and Esperanza and you—

KIMAYA

Don't you dare pretend that you did any of this for me. Valaria might have others fooled with that great martyr bullshit that she likes to talk, but she doesn't fool me and I know she doesn't fool you either. You put yourself at risk because you wanted to feel like a badass, and you put me and that kid sleeping in there and every other girl we know at risk, too!

RAPUNZELLE

Okay, first of all, that *kid* is a fighter, just like *every other girl we know*—

KIMAYA

She's a child! She deserves to have a normal childhood, and you and Valaria took that away from her—

RAPUNZELLE

Are you *joking?* We live on the Street of *fucking* Miracles. She lost the chance for the kind of normal life you're talking about before she was born.

KIMAYA

I've worked to give girls that chance for *fifteen years*—

RAPUNZELLE
(snorts)

Sure you have.

KIMAYA
(softly)

Just what are you saying?

RAPUNZELLE

Gimme a break, Kimmi. You swan around here, acting like
everyone's mother, always with the being *kind* and working
so *hard* for everybody *else* like goddamn Mother *Theresa*,
all condescending, and you call Valaria and me the mar-
tyrs? We did what we had to do for ourselves, and so did
the kid. You, you do what you do because you like control!

KIMAYA

Not. Another. Word.

RAPUNZELLE

Don't pretend like a part of you doesn't *love* that she's sleeping in your living room right now. Don't pretend like you
don't enjoy being able to say *I told you so* and act like her
frickin mommy, even though she was her own woman the
minute she first set foot on the Street of Miracles. Don't act
like half the reason you're mad at me is because Valaria and
I believed in her, because you felt like you couldn't control
her anymore, and the other half is because you can't control me anymore either!

A slap echoes like a gunshot through the alleyway.

KIMAYA
(breathing hard)

You're right. I can't control you, and I can't help you. No one can help you. Trying was my mistake.

RAPUNZELLE
Kimmi, come on, I'm not saying I'm not grateful you helped me get clean—

KIMAYA
No, you've made your point. You don't need to be grateful to me or anyone else.

RAPUNZELLE
So that's it? I have to be grateful to you or I don't love you?

KIMAYA
Just ... just stop, Rapunzelle. I'm tired. I'm tired of all of it.

A door opens and closes.

RAPUNZELLE
Me too, baby. Me too.

High heels click into the distance.

Mother to a hundred girls

If I couldn't sleep before, I definitely can't sleep after overhearing the drama between Rapunzelle and Kimaya outside. My head spins with all of the terrible and true things that each of them said, especially the part about girls who end up on the Street of Miracles being destined not to live normal lives. I mean, everyone already knows that, but aren't we supposed to hope for something more?

Or the thing about love and gratitude. And control. And Kimaya keeping control of girls by being kind to them. I never thought about that before, that being kind is a brand of violence all its own. And the thing is, I am grateful. I wouldn't have survived without Kimaya, her guidance and her gifts.

I hear her come inside, close the door behind her. She's breathing funny, like she's crying, and I kind of want to reach out to her, pull her into a hug, comfort her the way she's always comforted me, but I don't know now if that's the right thing to do. I don't even know if I know *how* to comfort anybody.

So I wait till I hear her lie down. Settle. I wait, counting backward from a hundred, until Kimaya's breath is slow and steady once more. And then I slide off the sofa bed, creep across the living room, and step into my shoes. I reach for the door and creak it open as quietly as possible.

"You going somewhere, my love?" Kimaya's voice cuts through the darkness.

Shit.

I turn around and see her standing across the room, just a silhouette against the wall. "Just going for a walk," I say, and I try to make my voice sound confident and nonchalant, but can hear it quaver. The shaking says, *can I trust you?*

Kimaya sighs. "You know, darling," she says, "I've played mother to a hundred girls. More, even. And I loved them, every single one."

Ghost hands run through my hair, stroking, soothing.

"Do you know how many of them have died out there? How many of them just disappeared, went out one day and never came back?"

"Kimaya," I say, "don't worry about me. I will always come back to you. I will always come back." And it's both the truth and a lie at the same time.

Kimaya waits, says nothing for a long moment.

"Go then, if you want to," she says eventually, "I won't make the mistake of trying to hold on to you too hard this time."

"See you soon," I say, and I mean it. So why is my throat clenched so tight?

And then, before either of us can say anything else, I turn and run out into the night.

How to catch a swarm of bees

It's a late hour to be visiting," says Alzena the Witch, when I get to her house covered in sweat. I have run all the way here.

"I need to know the answer to something," I say.

"Oh, honey," Alzena the Witch laughs, "you don't even know what the question is."

I swallow back a spike of anger, a spike of pride, the urge to slap Alzena in her witchy, bitchy, cryptic, know-it-all face. Ghost hands tug my wrists down, pry my fingers open.

"Three questions," I say, "then I'm done. I swear."

"Fine," she says. She doesn't look amused anymore. "But then you owe me something, too. A favour to be called in, at a time of my choosing."

I answer without thinking. "Fine. Is it true that girls who end up on the Street of Miracles are destined for violence?"

"You're destined for whatever your destiny is."

"That's not an answer," I snap.

"It's the only answer I can give you," she says, and I know I've wasted a question.

"Rapunzelle said that Kimaya helps girls because she

wants to control them. Is that true?"

"It's not a lie. Are these really the questions you want to ask?"

I lean in close. Look Alzena the Witch straight in her giant golden eyes. Searching for the words, the questions, the keys to unlock the doors to the things I want to know.

"How do you catch a swarm of bees?" I ask.

Alzena the Witch's face lights up. She laughs again, but this time she sounds truly joyful. She leans in as well, pushing her forehead against mine to scrutinize my face.

"With sweetness, of course," she says. "The same way you catch anything else."

from my notebook —

song of the pocket knife, part 6

after all this time,
it isn't you, it's me,
little silver pocket knife,
sweet razor smile
with your sharp true kisses,
you didn't let me down,
you've never failed me,
it's not your fault,
you couldn't cleanse me,
cure me,
forgive me,
love me,
i have to do those things
on my own.
and that is why, sweet knife,
i'm setting you free,
snapping you open and closed,
fluttering your wings,
offering you to the moon, a final taste
of my blood on your blade,
i'm setting you free,
releasing us both.

Baking the Forgiveness Cake

Sometimes, the world just won't stop spinning and spinning, unwinding itself like a spool of thread. Trailing strings of broken bodies and forgotten things through grey, empty space.

Sometimes, all you can do is lie on the sofa in your big sister trans girl's apartment and wrap yourself in blankets and barely, just barely, cling to life as nightmares swarm up all around you and killer bees roil inside your stomach.

At times like this, you feel your whole body shrivelling up like a giant starfish on dry land—all mouth and limp limbs and sand-encrusted skin. Full of your own salt and selfishness.

Times like this, you know beyond doubt that all you ever do is hurt things.

Yet, the world keeps spinning, a merry-go-round you can never get off. And somehow, some way, you find yourself circling around to a place you haven't been before, where all you can do is get up, drag yourself off the sofa, and stand in the shower under scalding hot water until you feel a little bit alive again.

In this strange new place, you feel the crushing weight of hopelessness so deep that it actually breaks you through to the other side, where anything might be possible.

This is where I am today: on the other side of hopelessness. On this day, I decide to bake a cake. To see if I can make something sweet.

To see if I can catch a swarm of bees.

It goes slowly, because I've never baked anything before in my life. Kimaya, who is of course an expert baker, keeps on running in and out of the tiny kitchen asking me if I need any help. I tell her that this is something that I have to do myself. Although I do let her give me a recipe to start off.

I think we're relearning how to be friends, Kimaya and I: she's taking care of me less, and I'm trying to take care of her more.

I begin by collecting the ingredients: Sugar, eggs, flour. Food colouring, cocoa powder, vanilla, butter, salt. Vegetable oil, frosting sugar, buttermilk, baking soda. When I read them aloud, they sound like a mantra. There is a subtle rhythm, a secret heartbeat under the words.

And then I begin: Opening packages and boxes and bottles. Setting out bowls and measuring spoons and whisks. Summoning the elements of creation. Pouring powders and liquids together to release the alchemy of transformation.

How did I ever think I could do this?

Time and the solar system collapse to the size of a postage-stamp kitchen. The single fluorescent light bulb hanging from the ceiling is the furious burning sun. The cramped vinyl countertop is the vast expanse of space. Beneath my wet, sticky hands are the dust and liquid that come together to form the primordial ooze, the raw goop from which life is made. I am She, the wretched Goddess with sweat-soaked hair, stirring the universe with a wooden spoon.

I crack an egg on the rim of a bowl: an atom splits and releases its blast. I whisk the ingredients and a planet is born. A chamber opens inside my chest, and salt water drips from my skin and my eyes to fall and vanish into the muck.

The world spins and spins.

I release a spoonful of food colouring into the mixing bowl, and an explosion of red overtakes all. Crimson, carmine, scarlet, vermilion. There is blood on my hands, blood in my batter. Sweet wet blushes stain my forearms, my palms.

The oven's thermostat dings. Fire roars inside its belly. I pour my batter into the cake pan, place it ever so gently inside. Close the door. Close my eyes to sleep and wait.

Eons pass. Years, decades, centuries flood by. Land masses shudder, oceans swell. The earth opens up to give way to new mountains. The world spins and spins.

The oven timer dings again. My eyes snap open. With a wave of terror, anxiety, ecstasy, I pull my cake out and into the world.

The cake is red. Red like flesh scraped raw after being thrown onto the pavement. Red like poisonous berries gathered by the side of the highway in the dark. Red like wanting the woman you love to answer your calls, open the window, accept your apology. Red like forgiveness.

The air ripples and shimmers around my cake as I pour honey and icing all over it. The scent of hot sugar diffuses in a thick cloud to fill up Kimaya's apartment, oozing into the cracks in the doors to spread lazily throughout the rest of the building, the block, the Street, the neighbourhood.

(Somewhere nearby, Rapunzelle raises her head off her pillow and sniffs at the air. The warm sugar smell tugs at her, pulling her up and into the Street.)

As I throw open the window and lift my cake up onto the sill, armoured insects rattle their sharp black legs in their labyrinthine hives under my skin. Ghost nails rake over my shoulders and back.

The world spins and spins. Sometimes, there is nothing you can do but surrender. There is nothing you can do but stand in your best friend's dingy kitchen and bake cakes and cry and hope hope hope for something better to come. Nothing you do will ever stop the world turning, will ever tilt the planet off its axis. All revolutions are futile in the end.

But.

I lift the fork to my mouth. The cake lands sugary and moist on my tongue, and a deep warm wet wave surges up in me. Something electric blasts through my bones.

I moan and close my eyes. Images blossom like fireworks against my closed lids. This is what I see:

In faraway Gloom, my little sister kneels alone in the trees behind our parents' house and opens her box of shells, mermaid scales, dried butterflies, and dead birds' wings. The wings and butterflies tremble, then rise up into the air, floating away. My sister follows them, ready at last to find where she belongs.

My mother, who is smoking out the back window, is suddenly struck by inspiration. She opens her mouth and begins to sing for the first time in twenty years.

Kimaya opens the door to the apartment. Rapunzelle is standing there. This time, she has no gifts, she has no words. She just stands there, looking her lover dead in the face. Kimaya opens her mouth to speak, then closes it. She sighs. Looks at the ground, then up again. She rolls her eyes, then puts her lips to Rapunzelle's.

Somewhere far away, Valaria is lounging against a stack of crates in an open-roof train car speeding through yellow wheat fields. She lifts her face to the sunlight pouring out of the blue, blue sky, and laughs.

Lucretia applies the finishing touches to her makeup. She looks in the mirror and, to her surprise, likes what she sees.

A brown-skinned woman is sitting at the counter of a corner store where she sells rice with lentils and lamb alongside the beer and cigarettes. She has not heard from her daughter in several months, although usually they speak on the phone for hours at least once a week. In her heart, she knows what has happened, has always been afraid it would. Very slowly, she opens the black-rimmed envelope that she received days ago. To her surprise, a green moth with extravagant wings flutters out. She closes her eyes and prays to God.

In a maze of catacombs hidden beneath the Street of Miracles, the vine-filled fountain containing the statue of the First Femme begins to rumble from deep within. The vines shift and twist, and water gurgles up between them to fill the fountain to its brim. The spirit of a dead policeman floats up to the surface and then speeds through the catacombs and bursts above ground. His need for vengeance fulfilled, he pauses once as he flies over the lanterns of the Street. Then he continues his way up, on his way to the next life, never to haunt my nightmares again.

In the kitchen, I open my eyes and cough once, twice, three times. A swarm of killer bees rushes out of my mouth and flies out the window. Sunlight pours through and warms my face.

Distantly, I hear the phone ring. As though sleep-walking, I pick it up. The boy from the University library is calling, asking for me.

The statue of the First Femme smiles.

A gentleman caller

Hey," he says, "it's Josh. From the library."

"Oh, hi," I say. "Yeah, I remember you."

"I hope this isn't too weird," he says, "but I guess I've been hearing about what's been going down with the police and all, and I was wondering if you were okay."

"Oh," I say.

He was wondering about me?

"Yeah. Um. So. Are you, like, okay?"

"Oh! Um. Yes," I say. "Sort of."

"Sort of," he laughs. "I think I know what that's like."

Really? Do you?

"Well, um, thanks for calling, I guess," I say. And then, to my surprise, "It's really sweet of you. I didn't think you remembered me, to be honest."

"Oh, of course!" he says, sounding cute and weird and nervous and adorable. "Of course I remember you." .

A warm, squirmy, tingly feeling moves up from the centre of my stomach and radiates outward through my chest and into my neck and face. I'm grinning like a middle schooler with a crush. Where are the bees, the killer bees, the swarming, buzzing army that has been with me for so long?

Gone for real?

Forever?

"Do you wanna hang out sometime," I say, all in a rush. Still no bees. No bees no bees no bees!

"Yeah," he says, and I can hear his smile. "I do."

Date night

And so it happens that in my eighteenth year, after running away from home, discovering my fierce femme tribe, joining a girl gang, accidentally killing a police officer, and baking a magical Forgiveness Cake, I am out on a date for the first time in my life with Josh The Blue-Eyed Library Boy.

What even is this *life?*

Kimaya was over the moon, of course. She wouldn't stop squealing "YES GIRL, GET IT" for over twenty minutes as she danced around the apartment looking for outfits for me. Which is why I am wearing this incredible red dress with plunging cleavage (even though I don't really have much to show yet) and black lace trim, glittery gold heels, and about fifteen pounds of makeup that make me look like an escapee from RuPaul's Drag Race.

I actually almost flaked out about thirty-seven times. As a concept, dates are terrifying to me. I think of them as carnivorous animals lying in wait in the shallows of a river, ready to leap up and plunge their enormous jaws into your neck and drag you off to the depths of a watery grave to be messily devoured.

Dates are dangerous, unknown entities. I kept

thinking: What does Josh want from me? What if he wants to go somewhere with bathroom attendants where they don't let girls like me in? What if he's one of those weirdos who thinks dating a trans girl is like some kind of act of charity?

What if it turns out that I'm really, really into him, and we want to jump each other's bones, but we can't because I'm so messed up about sex and my body and everything and he finds out that I'm this awful, violent, steaming mess of a person who turns everything she touches into horror and blood?

So yeah, I almost cancelled many times, but Kimaya went all Charlie's Angels on me when I told her, and she said she'd literally kick me out of the apartment if I didn't go on this date.

"Josh is an amazing person," she said. "If you don't go on a date with him, you will regret it for the rest of your life."

"Are you serious right now? I'll regret it the rest of my life if I don't go out with one guy? And what makes him so special anyway? What makes him any different from the thousands of assholes in this city who want a piece of trans girl ass?" I said.

"Well, for one thing, everyone in the femme community knows that Josh is a dreamboat," she said, rolling her eyes so that the tiny rhinestones on her false eyelashes shimmered and winked. "He's done all this great community work and writing. And for another, he's trans."

"That doesn't change anything," I argued.

"Maybe not," Kimaya said, "but you are going on this date, missy, if I have to drag you there myself!"

So I didn't flake out after all, and Josh comes to pick me up in his car (Who even owns a car? He's only like twenty-one, for god's sake!) at 8 p.m. like a gentleman out of a movie from the 1960s.

"You look amazing," he says, and the way he says it makes me kind of ... believe him. What is even happening to me? I'm not this girl, in a dress, in a car owned by a boy with blue eyes who goes to university.

This is someone's else's story, someone else's teen romance. Where's my weirdo punk transgender novel life gone?

"Thanks," I say, as he drives through the City. I'm trying to come off real casual, like I do this all the time. "So where are we going? What's the big surprise?" He had made a big deal on the phone about going on a "surprise adventure."

"Wellllll," he says, stretching the word out with a dopey grin and rubbing the back of his neck in an adorable awkward kind of way. "It's kind of weird, but I think you'll like it."

"Oh god," I say, "this is where I pepper spray you and jump out of the moving vehicle, isn't it?"

"No no no! This is actually good, I swear to you," he says. I raise an eyebrow at him, and he says hastily, "But if you really want to pepper spray me and jump out of the car, feel free at any time. Just let me know in advance, so I can pull over first."

"That's the sweetest thing any boy's ever said to me," I say, and although he laughs, it's kind of true.

He takes us through downtown, and onto a winding road that goes up the little mountain in the centre of the

City of Smoke and Lights. This mountain is a big tourist spot, and I'm expecting him to drive straight to the top, where there's a fancy restaurant where rich people go on dates.

But instead, he keeps on driving, into a heavily wooded area, until suddenly the trees clear, and we emerge into a huge, manicured landscape full of flowers and benches and carefully placed trees. And rising out of the ground at regular intervals are the shapes of angels...

"Are we in a *cemetery*?" I say. Who is this boy? How does he know me like this, already?

He blushes. "Yeah," he says, "my family has a mausoleum here, because my great-great-granddad was a founding member of the City or something. You'll see."

And right as he finishes speaking, he turns onto a side road, stops, and gets out of the car. He runs around to my side and extends a hand to help me out. He ushers me over to a section of the cemetery that's clearly reserved for rich people, because all the tombs are huge with elaborately carved angels and crucifixes and stuff, and several are covered with fresh flowers.

And there, in a little clearing surrounded by tall, blossoming lilac bushes, is a gorgeous stone shrine rising out of the earth. There's a little folding table and chairs set up beside it, with candlesticks and a picnic basket. Someone's strung up paper lanterns all through the lilacs, and the clearing glows with fairy lights.

"This is beautiful," I whisper.

"Really? Oh my god, that's great, because I wasn't sure if this was too weird or anything," he says, all in a rush. "I mean, I just had a feeling that this is the kind of thing you would like, and it's totally the kind of thing I like ... I mean, things that are sweet and kind of morbid all at the same time, but not, like, in a cheesy way, if you know what mean. I mean, do you really like it?" he asks.

"I mean, it's fucking weird," I say, and he laughs. It's a nice laugh, somewhere between a high-pitched giggle and a tenor chuckle. It's sweet and vulnerable and it makes me like him even more. "But it's perfect for me," I say. He looks me in the eye then, all bashful and amorous, and before I can stop myself, I lean over and give him a peck on the lips.

Is this me? My body, kissing a boy?

And there are no bees, no killer bees. No buzzing no jerking body no memories.

There is only me and a blue-eyed boy, the lilac bushes full of fairy lights, and the silent angel graves.

Orgasms, or, Giving up Ghost Friend

Blue-eyed boy, I can see your hands wanting to touch me. Your fingers—long, slender, clipped short at the nail—are shaking, just a little a bit, and it makes me like you more.

"Would it be okay if I kissed you?" you ask.

I laugh nervously.

"Um, okay. No worries! I, uh, I didn't, um. I mean, no pressure, I'm sorry, um..."

Blue-eyed boy, how can I tell you that my body is already promised to Ghost Friend? Already, I can feel their invisible fingers—cold, dry, immaterial yet tangible—tingling like chills all along the back of my neck, spreading along my shoulders, my spine. Gentle as ever. Sweet, sweet Ghost Friend. What am I supposed to say?

I lean over and kiss you, blue-eyed boy. Your lips are very soft and warmer than I expected. You kiss me back, sliding your tongue into my mouth a little bit. I lean into the kiss, put my hand on the back of your neck. The other on your waist. Ghost lips brush my collarbone as you slide a hand up under my shirt. I gasp. You stop.

"S-sorry," you stutter. "I guess, you're just not talking much, and I don't know what you want—"

I kiss you again, put my tongue between your lips. It's not that I don't want to talk, to tell you what I want. It's that I can't. My throat's a locked music box and the key's been thrown away. All my yeses and nos haven't been seen in years and years. I choke and gasp, breaking away from you. Tears sting my eyes. Even now, I can't do it. I can't let someone else touch me. I can't I can't I can't I can't I can't fuck this no I mean fuck me, yes please no I mean I don't know I don't know someone help me know what I want.

"Wait," I rasp, as you start to stand up, eyes full of concern. "Wait. Just ... just give me a sec."

"Okay," you say, looking totally freaked out. "No worries," you say, looking worried as fuck.

I close my eyes. Take a deep breath, lie back on the picnic blanket. Inside myself, I whisper, *Ghost Friend, are you there? One tap for yes, two taps for no.*

One tap. Ghost fingers massage my temples, smooth back my hair. A low, whistling sound like the wind picks up. You startle, looking around.

"It's okay," I say. "Don't be scared."

"I'm not," you whisper, looking terrified.

"It's okay," I say again, "I'm scared too."

Ghost Friend? Are you mad at me?

Two taps.

Even if I have to say goodbye to you?

One tap.

Do you still love me, Ghost Friend?

One tap.

Forever and ever?

One tap.

"You can touch my shoulder," I whisper, and although I'm talking to Ghost Friend, you hear me too.

"Okay," you say, and put a hand on my shoulder.

"You can touch my neck."

Your other hand starts to caress my throat. Ghost fingertips join yours, and I think you feel them, because I can see the surprise in your face.

"It's okay," I murmur, and the wind whistles again, long and low.

"You can take my dress off," I say, and two sets of hands slip my dress over my head.

"You can touch my breasts." The wind is louder now, moaning as you do.

"You can touch my stomach."

"You can kiss me again."

"You can touch my thighs."

"You can take your clothes off too, if you want."

"You can touch me *down there.*"

The wind blows louder and louder, as you explore deeper and deeper inside me. And then all of my hidden places are open, open, stories spilling out into the shimmering air, and we are coming, you and me both, and as the wind howls and the graves whisper and the clouds open, all of our ghosts fly up into the sky, free at last.

Dear Charity,

Well, what do you expect when you break a
boy's nose? You're right that he shouldn't have
grabbed you. Good for you, I guess.

So you've been watching the news, huh? Well, if
I was involved in any of that stuff, do you really
think that I could confirm it in a letter to my
thirteen-year-old sister? Yeesh, we'll never make
a criminal mastermind out of you, kiddo.

Seriously, though, all I can say is, I meant what I
said in my last letter: I can't protect you anymore,
Charity. I won't insult you anymore by trying to
pretend.

I live in a dangerous world. So do you. So do
all girls. I was wrong to try to prevent you from
growing up, from understanding that. I wanted
to protect you, but I'm starting to think that the
best thing you can do for people is teach them
how to protect themselves.

Every girl needs to be at least a little bit
dangerous.

But what I need you to understand, Charity,
is that you can't only be dangerous. You have
to keep room for softness in your heart, and for

sweetness too. Because knowing how and when to hit someone isn't going to save you from the darkness in yourself.

You can only stop hurting when you stop hurting yourself.

Love,

Your sister

ps: I'm putting a tube of my favourite lipstick into the envelope for your collection. The colour is called Scarlet Menace.

PART V: ESCAPE

The difference between hunger and love

Kimaya," I say, as we sit in her living room and pack my things for the move to Josh's place, "what do you think the difference is between hunger and love?"

It's been just six weeks since my first date with Josh, and it's like somebody cast a magic spell: I'm being whisked away into a whole new world full of nice furniture and freshly mowed lawns. As it turns out, Josh's parents are super-fancy rich professors at the University, and as a graduation present for getting his master's degree, they bought him an apartment in a nice area of town.

I actually met his parents for dinner last night. We went to a super-fancy restaurant for super-fancy rich people, where there were flowers and candles on the table. And the meal came in four courses, with food that was delicious but totally unrecognizable, and they paid for everything. Which is good because even though there were no prices on the menu, it was obviously very expensive. And delicious. I kept wanting to stuff everything into my mouth all at once, and had to consciously make an effort to eat slowly.

I was actually so nervous, I felt like I might throw up the whole time we were in Josh's car, driving to the restaurant. "Just be natural," he kept on saying. "My parents are super chill and down. They'll love you."

And they were actually pretty nice. Although I wouldn't say they loved me. Josh's dad just talked about Important Social Issues and made a lot of jokes that made Josh and his mom groan and that I didn't understand. His mom complimented my hair and outfit (Kimaya's work, of course), and then it kind of seemed like she didn't know what to say. And she flinched a little bit every time Josh went to hold my hand or touch my shoulder or something, so eventually I glared at him to make him cut it out.

And when they asked me what I *did*, I sort of just stuttered and said nothing.

Because I sure as fucking hell was not going to say, "Well, I recently ran away from home and was part of an all-trans girl vigilante gang until we accidentally killed a cop and our leader had to go on the lam. Speaking of lamb, this is delicious, by the way. Pass the salt."

And then Josh cut in and said, "She's actually a super-talented writer and is thinking about enrolling in the University soon to start a degree in creative writing," which made his parents give a big sigh of relief and start talking about all their favourite authors.

I guess that was pretty cool of him to do, step in and save me like that. Except. You know. Also kind of fucked up.

And now I'm going to move in with him, and he keeps on saying I should think about auditing classes at the University and probably I could get a scholarship and what a great writer I could be with my "gift for storytelling." And then I'll get published and become a superfamous Transgender Writer, and we'll get married and be a Transgender Power Couple, and have Transgender Children and raise them on a cloud of Transgender Happiness™.

And the thing is, I *want* that. I want it so, so bad. So bad I want to put it on a plate and stab it with a fork and stuff it in my mouth and down my throat until I hit that place deep down inside that has never, ever been full.

Hence the question: "Kimaya, what do you think the difference is between hunger and love?"

She looks up sharply. Takes my hand in hers. Maybe someday I'll play mother to a hundred trans girls of my own.

"Darling," she says quietly, "you are going to do a lot of things in your life. A lot of things you never thought you could. Just like every femme in the world, you have that gift. But you don't have to do anything you don't want to."

"But how can I know what I want?" I say, choking a little bit, because it hurts that she believes so much in me, my goodness, my *potential*, and I still don't, can't, won't.

"Every time I want something, I hurt somebody," I say so quietly, it comes out like a tiny thread of smoke from between my lips.

Kimaya still hears me. Sees me.

"Honey, you hurt yourself," she says, "because everybody around you hurts people and is hurting and that's just the story you were given. You can't get stuck in that. Don't get stuck in any one story, not even your own.

"That's the difference between love and hunger," she says. "Hunger is a story you get stuck in. Love's the story that takes you somewhere new."

What is this toilet paper made of?

It's the toilet paper that finally gets me, in the end.

Not the massive condo building made out of white cement and steel and glass with a security guard sitting at all times at a big white desk at the front entrance, or the fact that you need a magnetic card to get through any of the doors.

Not the in-building, full-sized swimming pool in the basement, equipped with a hot tub and steam room. Or the gym with its disinfectant smell and dozens of incomprehensible machines.

Not the chrome elevator, as bright and reflective as a mirror.

Not the giant glittering chandeliers that hang from the hallway ceilings.

Not the heavy oak door that opens into a vast carpeted open-concept living room about eleven times the size of my tin box apartment, furnished with tasteful leather couches, a glass coffee table that looks like a sculpture in a contemporary art museum, a state-of-the-art television, and wall-to-wall windows overlooking the City skyline.

Not the kitchen island, with its gleaming double fridge/freezer, dishwasher, double sink, and marble countertops that look like they've maybe never been used.

Not the bedroom with its sliding frosted glass doors and king-sized bed so big and so soft that it almost makes me cry the first time I lie down on it.

Not even the bookshelves brimming with every kind of book I've ever dreamed and never heard of.

All of that, I think I could have handled, you know? After all, it's the kind of place that everyone sort of wants to live in, has seen in movies about unhappy corporate executives, and secretly fantasizes about. So I was kind of prepared, in a way, for how everything looked and worked in Josh's apartment building. And he was so sweet and kind, in an embarrassed kind of way, as he led me inside and hastily explained, "This isn't my place ... It belongs to my parents, and the deal is I live here rent free and take care of the place and pay for any more school by myself."

Because that totally makes sense. To some people.

But you know, what I wasn't prepared for was my first moment alone in the apartment. Josh stepped out to get groceries to cook a "celebration dinner" for my moving in and I had to poop, so I went to the bathroom and sat on the thronelike toilet and wiped my butt with his toilet paper.

And it was the softest, silkiest, almost *sensual* toilet experience—like, something beyond imagining. Like nothing so, so *rich*, so heavenly, so luxurious, had ever touched my butt before. And I know it's ridiculous, but all I could think was, *What is this toilet paper made of? Did a hundred thousand silkworms die to make this roll?* There was no toilet paper like that in my house in Gloom, or on the Street of Miracles, I was pretty sure.

And it was this tiny thing, this insignificant experience, that finally made it hit me:

I don't belong here.

Full circle

So Josh came home and found his smashed-up TV this afternoon. I wanted to tell him that I didn't break it on purpose, it just kind of happened: I blew a kiss at the screen and the kiss was literally electric. But that would have just sounded like a lie to him. And maybe it would have been.

So I just said, "I'm sorry, Josh. I got angry and I needed to break something. I'll buy you a new one when I can get some money together."

He got this look on this face with his eyes all big and blue and sad and understanding and loving all at once. He held out his arms and drew me in. "It's okay, baby," he said, "it's okay. I'll take care of it. Don't worry about a thing." And he didn't sound mad, not even a little bit.

And that's when I knew it was time to run away again.

The greatest escape artist in the whole world

Oh, please. Don't look so surprised, now. You knew this was coming.

I told you from the very beginning, way back at the beginning of the book, that this was the story of how I became the greatest escape artist in the whole goddamn world. It is not the story of how I ran away from home like a little trans baby princess Cinderella, got rescued by a handsome transgender prince, and vanished happily into the vast palace of the middle class.

I'm packing my backpack right now, as we speak. Josh just stepped out to go to the University, so I'll have to make it quick. I'm not taking any money from him (well, not a lot—just a few bucks for the road), or anything else that belongs to him. Just a couple dresses, my heels, a notebook, and some other little things. Oh, and I have to remember to leave a note on his pillow to say thank you, and goodbye. And that I will never, ever forget him. The first living boy to give me orgasms.

Really? You still don't know why I'm leaving? Honey.

It's because I ran away to find myself, and so that I would never, ever be stuck in a story that someone else wrote for me. Because I said goodbye to my body full of bees and my heart full of ghosts, and now it's time to fill my body and my heart with something new. I'm putting on my short skirt and my candy-red heels, and I'm flying away to see if I know who I am, what I might still become, so I can find out how far I can get and if I can find my way back. Drawing a map of myself in the stars.

And there is nothing—not a swarm of killer bees, not a crooked house in a city called Gloom, not a blue-eyed boy and his sweet sweet kisses, not even a street full of beautiful sisters and violent miracles—that is strong enough to hold on to me forever.

I am leaving them so I can love them. I am going so that I can return.

Dear Charity,

I'm starting a new adventure. Sounds like
you are, too. Maybe we'll meet up on the road
somewhere. I sure hope so. Until then, take
care of yourself. I'm enclosing a pearl-handled
switchblade with this letter. Don't use it unless
you have to.

I will tell you everything—the truth, the whole
truth, nothing but the truth—someday soon, I
promise. I'm still just figuring out what exactly
the truth is, you know? Sometimes fiction is truer
than facts, and the trouble is knowing which
fictions are facts and which facts are fictions, if
you know what I mean. I'm not sure that made
sense, but whatever.

Someday, I'm going to gather up all of the stories
in my head. All the things that happened to
me and all the things I wish had happened. I'm
going to write them all down one after the other,
and I'll publish a famous best-selling book and
let history decide what's real and what's not.

Because maybe what really matters isn't whether
something is true or false, maybe what matters
is the story itself: what kinds of doors it opens,
what kinds of dreams it brings.

Yes, someday I'm going write things, all kinds of things, things that nobody's ever thought of before and things that they'll never believe: Stories about girls who run away to find out where Death lives and come back holding skulls full of fire. About girls who steal blood-red shoes and find themselves dancing with the devil till the end of time. About boys becoming girls and girls becoming boys and dangerous, violent people learning to find love in the dark at last.

I'll write it all: everything we were and are and are trying to become. I'll write for the girls who came before, and the girls who come next. For you and for me, for all of us dangerous girls.

Love,

Your sister

Acknowledgements

This book was written on unceded Indigenous territory. I am grateful to Ashley and Oliver at Metonymy Press for their interest in my work, incredible devotion, and amazing work ethic; as well as to Samantha Garritano for the astounding cover art. Thanks also to the RadStorm collective in Halifax, whose artist residency provided the space and time in which this book was born.

Without the work of many queer, trans, and racialized writers, this book would not be possible. I owe particular inspiration to Amber Dawn, Joey Comeau, Casey Plett, and Leah Lakshmi Piepzna-Samarasinha in this regard.

And then, of course, there are the trans women and trans femmes whose words, lives, and wisdom have so deeply shaped both *Fierce Femmes and Notorious Liars* and my life. May you consider this book my love letter to you all, an apology for the times that I have failed you, and a dream toward our future freedoms: Kama La Mackerel, Parker, Trish, Athena, Shahir, Betty, Gabrielle, Estelle, Morgan, jia qing, Avery, Autumn, Andi, Sophie, January, Amelia, Luna, Sebastien, and all the rest. My fists and my heart will always belong to you.

About the author

Kai Cheng Thom is a writer, performer, lasagna lover, and wicked witch based in Toronto, unceded Indigenous territory. She is the author of several award-winning works including the poetry collection *a place called No Homeland*, the children's book *From the Stars in the Sky to the Fish in the Sea*, and *I HOPE WE CHOOSE LOVE: A Trans Girl's Notes from the End of the World*. Her most recent publication is the picture book *For Laika: The Dog Who Learned the Names of the Stars*.